One
Wrong
Turn

Deanna Lynn Sletten

Also By Deanna Lynn Sletten

Miss Etta

The Women of Great Heron Lake

Night Music

Finding Libbie

Walking Sam

Maggie's Turn

Memories

Sara's Promise

Widow, Virgin, Whore

Destination Wedding

Summer of the Loon

Kiss a Cowboy

A Kiss for Colt

Kissing Carly

Outlaw Heroes

One
Wrong
Turn

Chapter One

Jessica Connors gripped the steering wheel as she maneuvered the twists and turns on Highway 1 along the Northern California coastline. It had been a rainy March day, and although the downpour had ended and the sun was peeking out from behind the clouds, the road was still slick. As she drove, Jess tried to concentrate on the road ahead, but her mind kept running through the list of things she still had to do that evening.

She shouldn't have tried rushing a drive into the city for groceries and paint, but their refrigerator was nearly empty, and she was eager to start painting the next bedroom. She had only two months left before the first guests arrived at their newly remodeled bed-and-breakfast, and there was still so much left to do. But her last-minute run up the coast had left her short on time to pick up the girls at school. Her seven-year-old, Jilly, would patiently wait for her in the hallway, probably playing a game of hangman or tic-tac-toe with Jerrod, the neighbor boy who carpooled with them. But Maddie, her twelve-year-old going on thirty, would be standing at the main door, arms crossed, with a sour frown on her face. Maddie didn't like having to wait for her mother, especially since her best friend, Emma, had to wait too. She thought it was rude when her mother was late. Well, she was right, but sometimes it couldn't be helped.

Increasing her speed, Jess took a turn a little too sharply, causing one of the grocery bags in the back of her small SUV to fall over. Damn! She hoped it wasn't the bag with the eggs in it. She knew she should slow down, but she was stressing over all that needed to be done. The groceries had to be put away, and they had to eat a quick meal before Jess took Jilly to swimming practice, where Jess was supposed to supply a healthy snack for fourteen girls. Then it was home and homework, and then—if Jess was lucky—she could begin painting the blue room after the girls were tucked in bed. In the morning, the rush to beat the clock would begin all over again.

It was hard being a single mom trying to start a new business and a new life.

As Jess took another curve, a lovely view of the beach below spread out before her. She sighed. They lived above a beach just like this one, yet she hardly ever had a chance to walk down the wooden steps to sit by the water and enjoy the tranquility. And once the B&B opened, she'd have even less time. But it had been her choice to abandon Los Angeles two years ago and bring the girls up here for a fresh start and turn her grandparents' home into a B&B. Though it had been necessary to begin all over again, the move hadn't been an easy decision. And it still wasn't easy. While she didn't necessarily miss LA, she did miss some aspects of her old life. She missed him. Especially him.

A strand of blond hair fell over her eyes, and she blew it away, all the while watching the road. Just as she rounded a sharp curve, a dog dashed out from the field on the left and into her lane. Jess turned the wheel sharply to avoid hitting it, but the wet pavement sent her car into a spin. Panicking, she overcorrected. The back end fishtailed halfway through its spin, causing the car to lose its grip on the road. The SUV tipped over on its side. Then, as if in slow motion, Jess felt it give way and roll. Her head slammed into the door frame as the driver's side hit the pavement, and the back door popped open, spilling the contents out onto the highway. The roof hit the pavement next with a sickening sound, like a pop can being crushed. Glass sprayed as the windshield shattered, and it rained over her. She reflexively squeezed her eyes shut against the flying glass. The car bounced back onto its tires, causing Jess to hit her head against the steering wheel. The momentum continued, and the car fell over onto the driver's side again, sliding along the opposite lane. The sound of the metal scraping on the pavement sent chills down Jess's spine. When the car finally came to a stop, it lay on the middle line, and Jess slowly opened her eyes. Through the shell of the windshield, she could see the road behind her. Blue and yellow paint had splashed in colorful trails along the road, and she thought how pretty it looked. A single shiny red apple caught her attention as it slowly rolled down the highway, and then all went black.

Chapter Two

Clay Connors pushed his unruly brown hair out of his face as he strode down the hospital hallway. His worn boots clicked on the shiny vinyl floor. He knew he was in desperate need of a shower and change of clothes, but there was only one thing on his mind right now. Jess.

He approached the nurse's station and spoke to the young woman who was working at her computer.

"Excuse me," he said hurriedly.

She stared at him, a bit startled, but composed herself quickly. "May I help you?"

"I was told that Jessica Connors is on this floor. Can you tell me which room?"

Hesitating, she studied him. He supposed the two-day growth of beard and his bloodshot eyes from lack of sleep weren't doing him any favors. "Are you a relative?" she finally asked.

"I'm her husband." The word rolled off his tongue so naturally yet felt strange. He hadn't referred to himself as Jess's husband in two years. But it was the truth, and if it would hurry the process along, he'd say it a hundred times. All he wanted was to see Jess.

The nurse typed something into her computer and studied the screen. She finally seemed satisfied with what she saw and stood up. "If you'll wait here a moment, Mr. Connors, I'll let the doctor know you're here." She didn't wait for him to reply before heading off down another hallway.

Sighing, he rubbed the back of his neck as he stepped away from the counter. Ever since he'd received the phone message that morning, all he could think about was seeing Jess. The hospital wouldn't tell him much over the phone except that she'd been in an accident and was in critical condition. Since then, all the worst possible scenarios had run through his mind. He had to see Jess with his own eyes to make sure she was still here, still alive. And God help him if she wasn't.

He silently berated himself for the hundredth time about not having his phone on all night. When he'd entered the recording studio yesterday afternoon to lay down some tracks, he'd turned the phone off so it wouldn't disturb his work. Then, a two-hour recording session turned into an all-nighter, and he hadn't thought once to check his messages. Why bother? Few people called him, and the only emergencies he'd encountered over the past two years were ones where a guitarist hadn't shown up at a session and he was needed immediately. But if only he'd pulled out his phone, just for a quick check, he'd have seen the hospital's messages about Jess. He could have hopped the early plane to San Francisco from LA and been here sooner. But by the time he'd seen the messages, after he'd returned home to his apartment, there were no planes until this afternoon. Unable to wait, he'd jumped in his car and driven instead. And now here he stood, waiting again.

He'd been awake now for thirty hours straight, and it was wearing on his nerves. He didn't think he could stand here one more minute without exploding.

"Mr. Connors?"

Clay turned. "Yes?"

"I'm Dr. Alan Bradbury," a tall man in a white jacket said, shaking Clay's hand. "I'm your wife's attending physician."

Clay nodded. *Just tell me she's alive.*

He stood there and listened as the doctor described Jess's head trauma, that a brain scan showed no signs of bleeding or tearing, but there was swelling that they were monitoring and giving her drugs for. Clay nodded, not quite understanding everything the doctor said yet thinking how terrible it all sounded. It was when the word *coma* came into the conversation that his mind became sharp again.

"Coma? Jess is in a coma?"

"Yes," the doctor said. "Sometimes, with a traumatic brain injury, it places the patient into a coma. We aren't too worried at the moment. A coma can be a positive thing. It allows the brain to heal and requires less oxygen to function than if she were awake. But as I said, we are continually monitoring her, and we are hopeful she will awaken in a day or two."

Staring at the man in front of him, Clay tried to grasp what was being said. "And if she doesn't wake up in a day or two?"

The doctor's expression stayed neutral. "Let's just take it one day at a time."

One day at a time. An expression Clay knew all too well.

He knew he wasn't going to get any guarantees out of this doctor, or any doctor for that matter. Experience had taught him that guarantees weren't something physicians were allowed to hand out.

"Our hospital is one of the leading trauma centers for brain injuries in the country, Mr. Connors," Dr. Bradbury assured him. "I promise we will give your wife the best care available."

Clay nodded. This was a lot for him to absorb all at once. "Can I please see my wife?" he asked.

"Of course." The doctor led him down the busy hallway to a room across from the nurse's station. There was a long glass window looking into the room, but a curtain pulled halfway around the bed blocked his view of Jess. Standing in the doorway, the doctor gave Clay his card. "Feel free to have the nurse summon me anytime you have a question."

Clay thanked him then turned his attention to the room.

He walked tentatively around the curtain. The sight before him made him stop midstep. Jess lay there with tubes and wires strung everywhere, the slow beep of a heart monitor keeping time with every beat of her heart.

Drawing closer, Clay felt his eyes well up at the sight of the woman he loved. The left side of her head was severely bruised, and there were stitches above her right eye. Small cuts were scattered around her face. Her beautiful blond hair was crushed against the pillow, and her eyes were closed. Lying on top of the blanket, both her arms were also streaked with cuts and bruises. IV tubes ran out of her left arm, and wires wound out from under her gown, connecting to the heart monitor.

Clay rounded the bed and dropped into the orange plastic chair. He reached for Jess's hand and held it ever so gently. "Oh, my Jess. My beautiful, precious Jess," he whispered, lightly stroking her hand. "I'm so sorry. So, so sorry. I should have been here. I never should have stayed away so long." Tears fell from his eyes, and he swiped them away.

As he held her hand, Clay thought back through the years. They'd been so in love, and yet he'd brought her so much pain. He'd never meant for it to be that way. Yet, through it all, he'd never stopped loving her. Carefully, he laid his cheek down on her hand and remembered the very first time they'd met. She'd been a spunky nineteen-year-old waitress, and he had been a twenty-four-year-old musician who was slowly making a name for himself as a lead guitarist. The bar where his band had played that night was small and crowded, close to the Redondo Beach Pier. Surfers occupied the seats, their girlfriends clad in little more than bikinis with T-shirts over them, but for Clay, there had only been one girl in the room—Jess.

* * *

June 2001

Clay stood on stage strumming an Eagles tune along with his four-piece band as suntanned guys with bleached mop tops and leggy girls danced in flip-flops on the floor in front of him. They were playing in a bar down the street from the Redondo Beach Pier, so both tourists and locals filled the room. This was the first time his band had played there—they'd played all over LA during the past four years—and he liked its vibe. The mood was laid back and the crowd was mellow. He'd certainly been in worse places.

Shaking back his long wavy brown hair, he caught sight of the cute waitress delivering burgers and beers to a table close to the stage. He winked at her and received an eye-roll back for his effort. Clay chuckled. She looked like a typical California girl with her blond hair, blue eyes, golden tan, and slender body that curved in all the right places. But he could tell she was no airhead beach girl from the smooth way she handled customers both good and bad. And the fact that she wasn't flirting with the band members made her even more interesting. Waitresses who paraded in front of the band were a dime a dozen. One who ignored them was unique.

The band played on—country rock, soft rock, the Beach Boys (duh!)—and the crowd shifted and changed throughout the night. The band took their breaks and began again. Once, while playing, Clay stepped down from the stage, and the waitress pressed past him.

"How about a beer?" he asked with a wink. She tossed him the best glare he'd ever received, but a few minutes later a fresh beer appeared on his amp, and he smiled wide. *Yep. She can't resist me.*

At one in the morning the bar finally closed, and the last of the beachcombers were shooed out the door. Clay and the band began packing up as the bar staff cleaned tables and swept the floor. He'd pulled his shaggy hair back with a leather tie to keep it out of his face while he worked. Once most of their equipment was loaded up, Clay headed over to the bar to get paid. As the manager counted out money from the till, the cute waitress came up behind the bar with a rack of clean glasses fresh from the dishwasher.

"Good crowd tonight, huh?" Clay said to her, leaning on the bar.

The waitress shrugged. "Lousy tippers, though."

"Well that wasn't nice of them. Pretty thing like you should have made great tips." He reached out his hand. "I'm Clay."

The waitress looked him over, making him feel self-conscious. Was his shirt sweaty? His jeans dirty? No one had ever made him worry about how he looked before.

Finally, she took his hand. "Jess."

Relaxing, he smiled. "Hi, Jess. What do you do for fun when you're not working?"

"I don't date band guys," she said bluntly.

He laughed. "Really? Is that all you've got? That's way too generic an answer for a smart-looking girl like you."

"Okay. I don't date guys with ponytails, either."

"Then you must not date much. Half the guys in this place had ponytails."

Jess stared at him, stone-faced. Clay wondered if he'd lost his touch with women.

"Here's your money," the manager said, handing him a wad of bills. "Can you guys play next Saturday night?"

"Sure. Be happy to," Clay said, and the manager walked off. Clay watched as Jess put away the last of the glasses. "Here," he said, pulling a twenty-dollar bill from the pile in his hand and setting it on the bar.

Jess stared at the bill and then back at Clay. "What's that for?"

"It's a tip. For the beer you brought me. And for the great conversation." He grinned.

Jess gave him a steely gaze before finally breaking into laughter. "Thanks."

He nodded. "See you next weekend."

She rolled her eyes, but this time with a smile.

* * *

A week later, Clay entered the bar with the other band members and began setting up the equipment. He kept an eye out for Jess, hoping she'd be there. He'd thought about her often over the past week, which was rare for him. He always said his first love was music and everything else came second. Yet the spunky waitress who couldn't have cared less about him had stayed in his thoughts. The confident way she moved around the bar crowd had impressed him, and her glare could stop the most hardened man in his tracks. But her sweet laughter at the end of the night when he'd joked with her had shown him her soft side. She enticed him to want to know her better.

Clay spotted her right before they started playing. She wore a short jean skirt with an apron over it and a yellow T-shirt. The yellow showed off her tan to perfection. Her blond hair was pulled up into a ponytail, and it swished back and forth as she walked between tables. Silently, Clay made his way behind her as she waited at the bar for drink orders to be filled. He tapped her on the shoulder. "Hey, pretty Jess. I'm back."

Jess twisted slightly to see who it was, rolled her eyes, and turned back to her work.

"Don't I even get a hello?" he asked.

Sighing, Jess turned, and as she stared at him, her eyes grew wide. "You cut your hair?" she said, clearly astounded.

Grinning, he gazed back at her. "Well, you did say you wouldn't go out with a guy who had a ponytail."

"You cut it for me?"

"Sure. So, maybe you'll say yes to that date?"

Jess stared at him a moment, then smiled mischievously. "We'll see." She picked up her tray full of drinks and strode off.

He laughed. Later that night, Jess's *we'll see* finally turned into a *yes*.

Chapter Three

"Excuse me, sir? Excuse me?" A sharp voice caused Clay to sit up suddenly. He rubbed one hand over his face as his other hand held Jess's. He glanced around the hospital room, dazed. Had he fallen asleep?

"Excuse me," the voice said again.

Clay caught sight of a woman standing in the doorway with two girls. The curtain was now wide open—when did that happen?—and the trio was staring at him. Recognition hit him as soon as he stared into the green eyes of one of the girls. Maddie. He looked at the other girl, and his heart flipped. Jilly-bear. They'd grown so much over the past two years that he almost hadn't recognized them. A smile slowly spread across his lips.

"Excuse me," the woman said again, shaking the smile from Clay. "Who are you?"

Clay stood, returning his gaze to the woman. She wasn't much taller than Maddie, and she was very thin, but her glare could knock a big man down to her size. She wore black pants, a stiff white shirt, and sensible flats. This was a no-nonsense woman. Frowning, he wondered why she was with the girls.

"I'm here to see Jess," he said, finding his voice.

"Who are you?" she asked again, circling her arms around the girls and drawing them closer, as if shielding them from him.

Clay opened his mouth to speak, but Maddie beat him to it.

"He's our father," she said tightly. She broke away from the woman's hold and walked stiffly over to her mother's bedside. The woman stared first at Maddie, then at Clay. She looked confused. But Jilly cocked her head, watching him curiously.

"Father?" the woman said. "I've known Jess since the first day she moved here, and she never once mentioned a husband."

Clay pushed down the annoyance that was rising inside him. "Well, I'm here now. The hospital called me about the accident, and I got here as soon as I could."

Maddie made a huffing sound. "Took you long enough."

Walking around to where Maddie stood, Clay kneeled down in front of her. He remembered when he could do this and they'd see eye to eye, but now she was looking down at him.

"Maddie. Sweetie. I'm sorry I didn't come sooner. I came the moment I got the message. I couldn't get a flight, so I had to drive. But I'm here now." He reached out to hug her, but she stepped back and glared at him.

His heart ripped open.

"Maybe I should take the girls home," the woman said, grabbing Jilly and waving Maddie to her. Still kneeling, Clay turned and saw the anxious look in the woman's eyes. *She doesn't trust me.*

Standing up, he tried to relax his tense face muscles. "Please don't leave. I'd like to see my daughters, and I'm sure they want to be with their mother."

He walked to the woman, offering his hand. "I'm Clay Connors."

The woman stared at his hand and then finally shook it. "Eileen Neilson. I live next door to Jess. We take turns carpooling the kids to school."

Clay smiled. "It's nice to meet you, Eileen. Thank you for watching the girls. I'm sure this has been a difficult time for them."

He dropped again to his knees and looked at his other daughter. They were almost eye to eye. "Hey, Jilly-bear. Will you give me a hug?"

The little girl stared at him a moment before tentatively stepping into his embrace. His heart danced at the feel of his daughter's small arms around him. When he pulled away, she was smiling at him.

Eileen watched him, still looking unsure. "I'm going to be blunt, Mr. Connors. How do I know there's not a restraining order against you? Maybe you shouldn't even be in this room with Jess or the girls."

His mouth dropped open. Did this woman think he was an abusive husband? A bad father? "I assure you, there isn't. I realize I haven't been around the past two years, but it was for other reasons. Jess and I are on very good terms."

Eileen crossed her arms and frowned.

"He's telling the truth," Maddie said. All eyes turned to her. "He's safe for us to be around."

Clay raised his brows, surprised but relieved that Maddie had spoken up.

"Well, okay," Eileen said. "If Maddie says you're fine, I'll believe her. But I'd feel better if I could take the girls home with me tonight until this is all settled."

Clay hesitated. He wanted to be with his girls. They needed him, and he desperately needed them if he was going to get through this tragedy. He had a lot of work ahead of him, rebuilding his relationship with both of them. Being apart this long had been difficult for them—and for him.

"I want to sleep in my own bed tonight," Maddie said. She looked over at Eileen. "It's okay, Mrs. Neilson. We can stay at our house with him." She turned her gaze on Clay, but it grew hard. "If he plans on staying."

Rubbing the back of his neck, Clay weighed his words carefully before answering. This was harder than he'd anticipated. Maddie's anger toward him was palpable, and he didn't want to make it worse by answering wrong. His throat was dry as he swallowed. It was tense times like these that brought on the craving for the one thing he couldn't have. The only thing that would calm his nerves and make him feel better. He pushed away that nagging urge, as he often had over the past two years, and spoke gently.

"I appreciate your concern, Eileen, but I'd like to have the girls with me. You're welcome to drop by the house anytime to check on them. They'll be fine. I promise you."

Eileen still looked unsure, but she conceded. "All right. I'll come by tomorrow morning to drive them to school. They missed today, but I think it would be good to get them back into their normal routine."

"I want to stay with Mom," Maddie blurted out. "I can miss school for a while."

Jilly ran to Maddie's side and slipped her hand over her mother's. "Me too," she said in a tiny voice. "Mom needs us."

Clay walked to the other side of the bed and gazed down at his two daughters. He knew how hard this was for him, but it had to be even more difficult for them.

"I think one more day off school can't hurt," he said gently, eyeing Maddie.

Glancing at him briefly, Maddie gave him a curt nod, then returned her eyes to her mother.

"Okay. Well, please let me know when the girls are ready to go back, and I'll be happy to drive them to school," Eileen said. Now standing at the foot of the bed, she gazed down at Jess. "Jess and I have become very close friends since she moved here. People around here like her very much. We are all praying for her quick recovery."

"Thank you," he said softly.

She reached into her purse and pulled out a business card, which she handed to Clay. "The girls have my number, but just in case, I'll give you this."

He looked at the card, which read *Neilson Contracting* with a phone number below it.

"That's our business. My husband's a contractor. You can reach me at that number too."

With a curt nod, she left, and his chest tightened. He was on his own with the girls.

Clay studied his daughters as they stood beside their mother. Both had changed so much since he'd last seen them. Maddie was taller and slender, her baby fat gone. Her brown hair had more red highlights, and it hung down past her shoulders in thick waves. Jilly was the exact opposite of her sister, with pale blond hair and blue eyes, and she still had that sweet face, so much like her mother's. She had only been five the last time he'd seen her, his little ball of sunshine with a quick smile and giggle. Clay knew that it was going to take time to make it up to them for being away. He hoped that they'd forgive him eventually.

After a while, he spoke. "Have you girls eaten?"

Both sets of eyes looked up at him. Both heads slowly shook from side to side.

"I haven't, either. Let's go down to the cafeteria and have something to eat. Then we can visit your mom again for a little while before we head home."

The girls nodded and filed out of the room.

The three ate their dinner in silence. Clay didn't want to push the girls to talk if they didn't want to. As he ate his sandwich, he watched each girl in turn, marveling at their differences and yet noticing how each one had small traits that reminded him so much of Jess. Maddie's eyes were big and round like Jess's, and she had her mother's long, slender legs. He could already tell that Maddie was going to be taller than Jess. Jilly's light hair reminded him of how blond Jess's hair used to get when she'd spend time in the sun, and her oval face was exactly like her mother's. He saw himself in each girl too. Maddie had inherited his dark, wavy hair and sullen temperament, while Jilly had his full lips and the dimple in her right cheek when she smiled. The same dimple he'd been teased for having as a young boy but which later made the women glance flirtatiously at him. But there was only one woman he wanted flirting with him now and forever, and right now she was lying in a room upstairs, fighting for her life.

Clay was exhausted by the time they returned to Jess's room. He'd been awake since yesterday morning, and his body was wearing down. He sat quietly across the bed from the girls as they took turns holding their mother's hand. Jilly told her mom she'd gotten 100 percent on her math test on Monday and that she and Jerrod had both been picked to be hall monitors for the week. Maddie stayed silent. She just sat there, staring at her mother as if willing her to wake up. From time to time she'd glare at Clay, then drop her eyes again. It was all so heart wrenching to watch, especially since his own heart was breaking at seeing his daughters so distressed. Finally, when the night nurse came in to check on Jess, he cleared his throat and suggested they go home for the night.

"I'll take good care of your mother," the nurse said gently, giving the girls an encouraging smile.

Maddie's and Jilly's faces looked drawn; both girls were clearly as tired as Clay felt. Neither argued as they picked up their backpacks and headed for the door.

Clay leaned over Jess and kissed her lightly on the forehead. "I love you," he whispered, then straightened up to see Maddie glare at him before storming out the door. Taking a deep breath, he followed.

* * *

They drove in silence all the way to the house. As they followed the coastal road, the sun set, trailing long rays of red and orange across the darkening water. It would have been beautiful to watch if not for the tension in the car and the thoughts running through Clay's mind. This was the road where Jess flipped her car.

As they passed over streaks of blue and yellow paint on the asphalt, Maddie spoke to no one in particular. "This is where it happened."

They all stared silently at the paint, each lost in their own thoughts. Finally, Clay broke the grim silence. "I'm sorry, honey. I didn't know this was the spot."

Maddie didn't say another word.

He tried not to think of Jess in the car as it flipped. Nothing seemed real. She had always been such a careful driver; it was difficult for him to believe she might have been going too fast or being reckless. Especially if she knew the girls were waiting for her. She loved her girls above all else. That was one fact he knew with certainty.

The old Victorian house loomed in the darkness as Clay made his way up the driveway. He'd no sooner put the car in park than Maddie was out the door and running up the steps of the front porch. Jilly got out slower and waited for Clay to grab his duffel bag and guitar case from the back before walking up to the house with him. Maddie had already opened the door, and the entryway light was on, spilling out onto the porch, guiding their way. As they walked over the threshold, Jilly turned and glanced at Clay as if making sure he was following. He gave her a small smile, and her face lit up with a grin. Closing the door behind him, he marveled at the beautiful oval of stained glass on the door. If that was any indication of how Jess had remodeled the old house, he knew he was in for a treat.

Standing in the entryway of the four-story house, Clay looked all around. Directly in front of him was a staircase leading up to the second floor. It had shiny mahogany bannisters that swirled at the ends. Jess had refinished the wooden steps and placed a soft gray-and-white carpet runner up the center. A hallway beside the staircase led to the back of the house, where there was a small bedroom and an entry into the kitchen.

To his left was the formal dining room, which held a polished mahogany table that could seat twelve and had belonged to Jess's grandmother. A hutch filled with china sat against one wall, and there was a matching sideboard on the other. Jess had painted the original wainscoting a soft cream color and added fresh wallpaper that had a red rose pattern above it. Under the table sat a vintage Turkish rug of faded red, black, and tan hues. A heavy swinging door was on the far wall and led to the kitchen.

To his right was the living room, or parlor, with a large

fireplace and a seat in the bay window. A round rug in soft tan shades covered the hardwood floor, and a cream sofa was positioned in front of the fireplace with a coffee table in front of it. Wing chairs flanked each side of the sofa, and two groupings of chairs were placed in other sections of the room to create pockets of privacy. Clay loved that Jess had forgone the typical use of Victorian-style décor for a B&B and instead had used light colors to keep the rooms airy. And although everything looked lovely, it was the outline of an old upright piano that brought a smile to Clay's lips.

"I'm glad to see your mother kept the old piano," he said, looking over at the girls. Maddie had one foot on the staircase, and Jilly was standing near her, watching him.

"How do you know about the piano?" Maddie asked. "You've never been here before."

"Yes, I have," he said, setting down his duffel bag. "I came up here with your mom to visit her grandparents before you two were born. Your grandmother played that piano every day. She had a real talent for it."

"Maddie plays too," Jilly offered, but was given a dirty look from her sister for her effort.

"Maddie, you still play?" Clay asked. "I'd love to hear you play something."

Maddie frowned. "I don't play anymore," she said stiffly.

Jilly looked at her quizzically. "What do you mean? You play in the middle school orchestra."

Maddie nudged her. "Let's go to our room, Jilly," she said, waving her sister upstairs. Jilly turned and silently followed.

Clay picked up his bag again and headed up the stairs behind the girls. He was exhausted and couldn't wait to crawl into bed. The emotions of the day, from the moment he'd learned about the accident to the cold way Maddie had received him, had been more than he'd thought he could take. His nerves were frayed and raw. He hoped that sleep would calm him and get him through what he was sure would be another stressful day tomorrow.

They walked up the stairs all the way to the attic. "Why are we going way up here?" Clay asked.

"This is our living space away from guests," Maddie answered. "Our room, Mom's, the bathroom, and our own sitting room. The other rooms in the house will be for guests."

He nodded. The ceiling was tall and flat here, but he knew the bedrooms on either side would have slanted ceilings. The girls headed through the sitting room and went into a bedroom that held two twin beds. He headed for the room on the opposite side. Opening it, he knew right away that this was Jess's room by the soft scent of lavender. Memories of Jess rushed past him as he inhaled her favorite perfume. Their first date, the first time they kissed, the night they made love under the stars. His heart swelled with love as he remembered it all.

"What are you doing?" a sharp voice said, interrupting his thoughts. Clay turned.

"You can't sleep in there. That's Mom's room," Maddie insisted, her green eyes flashing.

"I'm sure your mother won't mind," he said.

"No! That's not your room!"

Clay was taken aback by the sheer outrage in her tone. The last thing he wanted was to upset the girls tonight. "Okay, that's fine. I'll sleep in one of the bedrooms downstairs," he said.

Maddie strode into the middle of the sitting room. "You can't do that. The rooms that are finished are for guests. You'll mess them up. Mom worked really hard on them."

Running a hand over his face, he tried to stay composed. He had to hold it together. This was a difficult time for all of them, and getting angry at Maddie wouldn't help. "Tell me where I can sleep, then."

Maddie looked unsure. There was a sofa between them, but it wasn't long enough for Clay's tall body to sleep on. He decided to take matters into his own hands. "There's a sofa downstairs in the living room. How about I sleep there tonight?"

Maddie took a moment to think this over. "Fine," she said. Turning, she stormed past Jilly into their bedroom.

Clay sighed, then forced a smile for Jilly, who was still watching him. "Good night, Jilly-bear," he said, then headed back down the stairs.

Stepping into the living room, he snapped on a lamp beside the sofa. He was so exhausted that he didn't care if he had to sleep on the floor—he knew he'd fall asleep as soon as he lay down. He dropped his duffel bag and carefully set his guitar on the floor out of the way. As he stood up, he heard a small sound in the entryway.

"Dad?"

He turned. There stood Jilly, her arms filled with sheets, blankets, and a pillow.

"You'll need these," she said shyly.

Clay's heart melted. He walked over and took the bundle from his daughter's arms. "Thanks, sweetie."

Jilly gave him a quick nod and scurried up the stairs.

Thank goodness one of his daughters was on his side.

Quickly, he made up the sofa with the bedding, slipped off his boots, and crawled under the blankets with his clothes on. The last thing he remembered before dropping off to sleep was the sweet scent of lavender and Maddie's flashing green eyes.

Chapter Four

June 2001

Clay and Jess cruised along the curvy coastal road in his battered pickup truck, with the windows wide open and the Eagles blaring over the speakers. They stopped at a little burger joint tucked away a block from the beach and sat at an outside table under a striped umbrella. It had been a beautiful day, and even now, as the day was winding down, the weather was perfect.

After ordering, Jess looked at him curiously. "So, how do you know about this place?" she asked.

"Played here a few times. They have a small stage in the back corner where we barely fit. But the place brings in a good crowd."

"Do you play at all the little bars in the area?"

Clay grinned. He liked that Jess was interested in his band. She looked so adorable tonight wearing a red tank top under a white cotton shirt that she'd tied at the waist of her faded blue jeans. Her blond hair hung loose, and she kept slipping it behind her ears. He thought the splash of freckles across her nose and cheeks was cute. He could barely believe he'd talked her into going out with him. She was much too good for a lowly band guy like him.

"We play anywhere they'll pay us to," he told her. "I've been doing this since high school, so I've been in a lot of little dives up and down the coast."

Jess gave him a sly look. "And do you ask out every girl you meet in those little dives?"

Clay shook his head. "Actually, no, I don't." Seeing the surprised look on her face, he continued. "I take playing music seriously. When I'm not playing with the band in a bar, I'm at the studio either playing background tracks for other artists or hoping to. Last year, I was on the road for six weeks playing lead guitar and singing backup for an up-and-coming country singer. I've been so busy lately that I haven't had time for a social life."

Jess cocked her head. "So, why me?"

Leaning in closer to her, Clay propped his elbows on the table. "You were too cute to resist." He grinned.

"That's it?" She rolled her eyes. "California is packed full of cute girls. There has to be more to it, unless you're giving me a line of bull."

Before he could answer, their burgers and fries came. After the waitress left, Clay took a bite of his burger, chewed slowly, then looked seriously at Jess.

"You're right. There was something more. Girls who flirt with band guys are a dime a dozen, but you had no interest in any of us. You were there to do your job and not to mess around. I liked that. You piqued my interest."

"Hmm. Well, that sounds like an honest answer. Do you know how tired I get of band guys coming into the bar and asking me out? And most of them aren't serious musicians like you seem to be. I've learned how to blow them off."

"So, why did you say yes to me?"

"How could I say no? You cut your hair for me. I figured you must have been serious about going out with me if you'd cut your hair to prove it."

He laughed and Jess joined in. They ate in silence for a while until Clay spoke up again. "So, what's your story? You know I'm a musician, but what about you? I highly doubt your life ambition is to be a waitress in a bar."

Jess gave him a small smile. "No, waitressing isn't my dream, but it's a good way to earn money for now. Actually—and don't you dare make fun of me—I'm saving to go to school next year."

"Why would I make fun of you? I think it's great you're planning on going to college."

She looked sheepish. "I'm not exactly going to a regular college. I want to go to pastry school."

"You mean like baking?"

"Yes. I love to bake, but I want to learn to do more than just the basics. I think it would be fun to create beautiful desserts."

"What made you fall in love with baking?" he asked.

Her face glowed. "I think it started when I was very little. My mom worked all week long, so on weekends we'd bake cookies or cakes together. She had one of those old cloth pastry bags where you attach the different tips, and she'd let me decorate cakes and cupcakes with it. It was our way of spending time together. And as I grew older, our creations became more complicated, and I realized how much I loved learning to make new desserts. My high school friends liked it too. They were my taste testers."

Clay grinned. "Lucky them. Can I taste test all your tasty treats?"

Jess giggled. "We'd better still be talking about baked goods here," she said, making him laugh. "We'll see if you're still around when I finally get to it."

"Hey, you're not going to get rid of me now. With all those great desserts? I'm there." They laughed and then left the restaurant and drove the short distance to the beach. The sun was low in the sky, and they took off their shoes and walked along the water's edge on the hard-packed sand. After a time, Clay reached for Jess's hand and held it as they walked. She didn't resist, which made him happy. It was almost sunset by the time they made it back to the truck.

"Wait here," he said, and then he went to the truck and returned with a small cooler in hand. He led her to a quiet spot where they could watch the sunset, then reached into the cooler and handed her a bottle of beer.

She looked at him a moment, seeming unsure. "I'm only nineteen," she said.

"You've never had a beer before?"

"I didn't say that. I'm just warning you that I'm underage."

He chuckled. "Well, as far as I'm concerned, if you can serve the stuff, you can drink it too. Don't worry, I'll only let you have one."

She took it, and they sat side by side, watching the sun touch the water and turn it a brilliant reddish-orange color.

"I had fun tonight," Clay said, looking at Jess. She gazed back at him, and her eyes were sparkling in the fading light.

"Me too."

"Do you think we can do this again sometime?"

She smiled. "Sure."

As the last rays of the sun faded into the ocean, Clay bent down and kissed Jess lightly on the lips.

* * *

Bang! Bang! Bang! Clay woke suddenly from his dream to a loud rapping noise. He shook the sleep from his head and glanced around, confused for a moment before remembering where he was. Bang! Bang! Bang!

"Who in the hell is making that racket?" he said as he picked up his phone and looked at the time. It was eight thirty in the morning. "Cripes!"

Bang! Bang! Bang!

He finally realized someone was knocking on the door. Untangling himself from the sheet, he stumbled across the room. Jerking the door open, he saw Eileen standing there, a bag of groceries in one hand and a gallon of milk in the other. A large cloth bag hung from her shoulder.

"Did I wake you?" she asked, giving him the once-over.

He stared at her blankly, unable to comprehend how anyone could be wide-awake and crisply dressed this early in the morning.

"Yes, I was sleeping. Yesterday was a long day," Clay said, trying not to sound rude. Realizing how disheveled he must look, he ran his hand through his hair. He doubted that it helped.

"I picked up the girls' homework for them this morning. And I brought a few groceries too," she said, stepping into the entryway and handing the bag and milk container to Clay. "I figured you must be almost out of the basics. Jess had groceries in the car when she had the accident."

He realized he didn't know many details about the accident. It felt strange that the neighbor knew more than he did. But then again, she'd been here and he hadn't.

"Thank you," he said. "I'll put these in the kitchen."

"Where are the girls?" Eileen asked, glancing around. "I can give them their assignments."

"I'm sure they're still asleep," Clay said.

"Asleep? Really?" She appeared shocked, as if sleeping in on a weekday was a mortal sin.

"Hi, Mrs. Neilson," Maddie called out as she pushed open the kitchen's swinging door and padded through the dining room. Jilly followed her. They were both awake and dressed. Clay wondered why he hadn't heard them get up.

"Oh, there you are," Eileen said, sounding relieved. "I brought you milk and cereal in case you'd run out. And your teachers gave me your homework." She handed Maddie the cloth bag she'd had over her shoulder.

Maddie didn't look thrilled about the schoolwork but thanked her for bringing it. "We do need milk. Jilly and I used the last of it for breakfast."

They already ate breakfast? And I didn't hear them? Clay knew he'd been tired, but he must have been dead to the world.

"Well, I'll be on my way," Eileen said, seeming satisfied that the girls were still alive and well.

"Thank you again for the groceries," Clay said as he followed her to the door. "I can pay you for them."

Eileen looked insulted. "Don't worry about it. It's the least I can do for my friend. I may see you later at the hospital. I plan on dropping by to check on Jess."

Nodding, he said good-bye. He turned to the girls. "Good morning. I didn't know you were up already. I was sleeping pretty heavily, I guess."

Jilly giggled. "You were snoring. Like an old grizzly bear."

Clay laughed. "Yeah, I guess I do that."

Maddie didn't look amused. "When are we leaving for the hospital?"

His smile faded. "Let me grab a shower, and we can be off. I'll put these away first." He headed into the kitchen, then stopped short. When Jess's grandmother had lived here, the kitchen had been old and tired, with white appliances from the 1970s and faded wallpaper with big orange flowers on it. But now he was standing in a newly remodeled kitchen with oak cabinets, quartz countertops, and stainless-steel appliances.

It looked bigger and had more cabinets and counter space than before. A sliding glass window had also replaced the small windows on the far wall, allowing the sun to light up the space. Clay turned to the girls, who'd followed him in. "Wow, your mom did a nice job on this kitchen. This is beautiful. And more spacious."

"Mom's been working really hard," Maddie said. Clay thought it sounded more like an accusation about his not being here to help than a compliment to her mother.

"Yes, I can see that," he said, choosing to ignore his daughter's tone. He put the milk away in the fridge and pulled the groceries out of the bag. He hesitated, not sure where to put things.

"The cereal goes up in that cupboard," Jilly offered, pointing to the spot.

"Thanks, Jilly-bear," Clay said. Eileen had also bought baby carrots, apples, bread, butter, and yogurt, so he put those away in the fridge.

He turned to the girls. "If you don't mind, I'll go upstairs and shower."

Maddie frowned. "That's our bathroom."

Clay took a deep breath. Maddie was battling him at every turn, and it was gnawing at his nerves. He didn't want to fight with her, though. It would only make things tougher. "Okay. Then where should I shower? I can't go to the hospital looking like this."

Maddie wrinkled her nose. "There's a bedroom and bath-room in the back of the house—behind the kitchen—that Mom said was originally built as a maid's quarters. She's keeping it empty in case she hires help. You can use that room."

Wow, I've been relegated to the maid's quarters by my daughter, Clay thought. It wasn't worth arguing over, though. At least he'd have a place to stay.

"The maid's quarters it is," Clay said, walking past the girls and into the living room. He picked up his duffel bag and walked to the back of the house. To the left was the bedroom, and off the back was a large screened-in porch. Beyond that was the backyard, with its apple and pear trees and plots where flowers grew every year. *At least I have a nice view.*

The room was small, and so was the bathroom, but it was serviceable, and soon he was clean-shaven and showered. He slipped on a pair of jeans and a cotton plaid shirt over a black tee before pulling on his boots. When he looked in the mirror, he saw a semi-respectable man looking back at him—except for the shaggy hair—but inside he felt in turmoil. He had hoped a good night's sleep and a shower would calm his nerves, but he still felt on edge. The stress of Jess's accident and medical condition, along with Maddie's angry reception, had really done a number on him. He needed to do something quickly before he came undone.

Clay picked up his phone and dialed his friend Cooper James, a bass player he'd known for twenty years. He was also his AA sponsor. Coop answered on the second ring.

"Hey, man. Good to hear from you. How is Jess doing?"

Clay had texted Coop yesterday about Jess's accident.

"Not very well, I'm afraid," Clay told him. "She's in a coma from a head injury. The doctor put a positive spin on it, saying it's how her body will heal. So I'm hoping he's right."

"Sorry to hear that. I hope she comes out of it soon. How are the girls? Were they happy to see you?"

Clay sighed. "Well, Maddie isn't too happy with me, but Jilly is warming up. Can't blame them, though. They haven't seen me in two years."

"Might be a good time for an amends, eh?"

"Yeah. I plan on it," Clay said.

"Good. Now, how are you holding up?" Coop asked.

"Not too well. My nerves are about shattered. That's why I'm calling. Can you check if there's an AA group nearby? Even if I have to drive into the city, I will. But it would be easier if one was closer."

"I'll check on it for you, bud, and text you the location. Until then, hang in there, okay?"

"I will. Thanks, Coop."

"I'll keep Jess in my prayers."

"Thanks, man. She needs that," Clay said. He wasn't much of a praying man himself, but he'd take whatever he could to bring Jess back to him.

"I know this is a difficult time for you, Clay, but it's time you step up. Jess needs you now more than ever. She and the girls. This is what you've been working toward for two years. You can do this," Coop told him.

Clay took a breath. He knew Coop was right, but it was so much responsibility, so quickly. "I'll try. One day at a time, right?"

"Yep. One day at a time," Coop said.

After they hung up, Clay thought about Coop's words: *It's time you step up.* He knew Coop was right. In fact, Clay should have stepped up months ago. If he had come back to Jess and been here for her and the girls, maybe she wouldn't be lying in the hospital unconscious.

"Thoughts like that aren't going to make this easier," he said to himself. Standing up, he straightened his shoulders and steeled himself for whatever the future brought his way.

Chapter Five

They rode in silence the entire forty-five minutes to the hospital, as they'd done on the way home last night. No amount of prodding by Clay could get Maddie to speak, and Jilly stayed quiet as if out of loyalty to her sister. He glanced in the rear view mirror to gauge the girls' reactions as they once again passed the dried paint on the asphalt. Both sets of eyes stared at it, but neither girl said a word. The stillness in the car afterward felt even heavier.

He stopped at the nurse's desk before going to Jess's room. Maddie wanted to head directly to her mom's room, but Clay made her wait. She crossed her arms and glared at him, but he didn't give in. He wanted to make sure no one was in there doing any type of procedure on Jess before he took the girls in. The nurse gave him the all clear and said she'd let the doctor know he was there.

When they entered the room, the girls immediately set their backpacks down and ran to their mother's side. Clay walked around to the other side of the bed and gazed down at Jess. Seeing her today was not as shocking as it had been the first time. Her hair was clean and brushed, lying smoothly against her pillow. The bruises on her face and arms had turned a dark purple, and the cuts were showing signs of healing. Besides that, nothing had changed. Jess was still in a coma.

"Your mom looks better today," he said, trying to sound optimistic. "The nurse must have washed her hair."

Maddie glanced up at him but didn't respond.

Jilly gently took her mother's hand. "Yeah. She looks nice today," she agreed.

Maddie pulled a chair over for Jilly, and the girls sat together beside their mother. If Clay had been alone with Jess, he might have talked about memories they'd shared and how much he'd missed her these past two years. But he wasn't sure how Maddie would react to that, and he didn't want to upset her right now.

"You should talk to your mom, Jilly," he said tenderly. "Like you did last night. I've heard that people in comas may actually be able to hear everything going on around them."

Jilly looked at her dad. "What should I say? I told her everything yesterday."

"Well, you could tell her simple things, like if you slept well last night, what you ate for breakfast, or how nice the weather is today. Anything, really. Just let her hear your voice." Clay turned to Maddie. "And your voice too, Maddie."

Maddie didn't even look up to acknowledge that he'd spoken.

Jilly started talking softly to her mother. "Mom, me and Maddie are okay. I know how much you worry, but I don't want you to. That way you can get better faster. Maddie helped me with breakfast this morning and poured my milk. I didn't want to spill it all over and make a mess. And Dad's here now. He can take care of us until you come home." She glanced over at her dad, and Clay smiled at her. This seemed to encourage her to go on. "I'm glad Dad's here. Maddie isn't too happy about it, but I don't mind."

"Jilly . . . ," Maddie said in a warning tone. "Don't tell Mom that."

Clay tried to keep a straight face, but it was hard. He looked down at his lap so the girls wouldn't see him grinning.

Jilly glanced over to Maddie. "You say something to Mom."

Maddie's eyes turned to Clay, then back at Jilly. "Not now."

Clay knew Maddie wouldn't say anything as long as he was in the room. She kept her feelings very close to the vest and wasn't about to look vulnerable around him.

His cell phone buzzed, and he glanced at it. Cooper had found a local AA meeting for him to attend. It was at seven tonight in the local Lutheran church basement. Relief flooded over Clay. A local meeting would be easier to attend, and he really needed to go to one before he totally lost it.

Dr. Bradbury came in a while later, and Clay went out into the hall to talk to him. The girls had taken out their school assignments by then and were sitting beside the bed working on them. Clay was thankful that they had something to concentrate on other than their mother's situation.

"How is she doing?" Clay asked.

"All signs show that your wife is healing fine. The brain swelling has gone down, thanks to the drugs, and her heart and lungs sound good. We're pleased with how well she's doing at this point," Dr. Bradbury said.

Clay frowned. "But she's still in a coma."

"Yes, but this is only the third day. She could wake up at any time. We just have to be patient."

At that moment, being patient wasn't one of Clay's strong suits.

When he reentered the room, both girls looked up at him expectantly.

"What did the doctor say?" Maddie asked.

He took a deep breath. He wanted to sound upbeat, despite feeling the opposite. It seemed to him that if Jess was doing fine, she'd be awake. "The doctor said your mom is doing well. He said we have to be patient and see how things progress."

Maddie gave him a sour look. "If Mom's doing so well, why isn't she awake?"

Clay deflated like a pinpricked balloon and sat heavily in the chair. "I don't know, Madds. I'm repeating exactly what he told me. That's all we've got for now."

She stared hard at him a moment, then returned to her schoolwork. Jilly's face, however, was a mixture of emotions. She looked like she was trying to be strong like Maddie, but her lip quivered, and her eyes glistened with unshed tears. She raised those eyes to Clay, and his heart melted. All it took was a nod of his head, and she came flying into his arms, letting the tears fall.

"Is Mom going to be okay?" she asked into his ear as she wrapped her arms around his neck.

Clay held her tightly, his heart filled with love for his little girl. Being away for so long, he'd forgotten what it felt like to have small arms hold him in such a loving embrace. Swallowing the lump that had formed in his throat, he said, "The doctor is doing everything possible to make sure she'll be fine, sweetie. We have to hold in there. Believe me, I want her to wake up as much as you do."

"Why? So you can leave again?" Maddie said sharply.

His mouth dropped open at Maddie's spiteful words. Jilly pulled away and stared at him, her eyes wide, clearly wanting him to reaffirm that he was staying. He could see it in those deep pools of blue.

"I'm not going anywhere," he said softly to Jilly, seeing the relief in her face. "I'm staying right here," he said, louder and more determined, looking over Jilly's shoulder at Maddie. But all he got for his effort was Maddie wrinkling her nose and returning to her schoolwork.

Jilly, still in his lap, drew closer and whispered in his ear, "I believe you."

"Thank you," he whispered back. Then she climbed down, wiped her tears away with her sleeve, and went back to her chair and her schoolwork.

In those few moments, Clay had been through the gamut of emotions. Stress was his enemy. It tempted him do the one thing he shouldn't. His nerves were stretched thin, making him wonder how he'd even make it through the day.

The hours wore on. Nurses came and went, offering comforting smiles. Maddie read, and Jilly worked on word puzzles for extra credit. In the silence, Clay had too much time to think. He gazed at Jess, wondering what he'd do if she didn't wake up. He knew he should think positive thoughts, but he also had to contemplate the future. How could he, a musician who worked odd hours and sometimes went on the road for weeks at a time, provide a good home for his girls without Jess? Who could he trust to watch over his daughters? And what did he know about raising two girls anyway? Jess had always taken care of the day-to-day matters with the family. What if he screwed up? Or worse, what if he started drinking again? Just thinking about it scared him to death. But he knew one thing for certain—he'd never leave his girls again.

He replayed the past two years in his mind, wondering how he'd been able to let the time go by without seeing them. He understood *why* he had, but it seemed like such a lame excuse now that he was with them. He hadn't planned on being away this long—it had just happened. After his last stint in rehab, he'd been determined to go back to Jess and the girls and try once again to be a family. But after living in a sober house for two months, he had decided he still needed more time. By then, Jess had moved the girls up north, and their LA house had been sold. He'd rented a small apartment, thinking it was only tempo- rary. One day at a time. That was his mantra. First, he'd started working again, slowly picking up studio jobs until his schedule was full. He'd stayed away from playing live in bars or on the road. He knew that would be too much for him to handle. As the weeks went by, and he was able to work and stay sober, he'd told himself he would soon be able to return to his family. But weeks had turned into months, months into years. Every time he thought he was ready to add his family back into his life, he'd panic and put it off. What if he returned to them and couldn't stay sober? Was that fair to Jess? The girls? So he would put it off longer, just to make sure he could maintain his sobriety. But two years? How could he have let that happen? It was no wonder Maddie couldn't stand the sight of him.

At noon, they went down to lunch in the cafeteria and then returned to Jess's room. Nothing had changed with Jess. She just lay there, and the silence continued to swell between Clay and the girls. When Eileen dropped by at one, it was a huge relief for Clay to see her.

"How's she doing?" she asked.

"The same, I'm afraid," he said. "But the doctor said it's only the third day and that we shouldn't worry."

She nodded.

"Can I speak to you in the hall a moment?" he asked.

"Okay." Eileen turned and headed out of the room.

"I'll be right back," Clay softly told Maddie, who was still reading her book. Jilly had fallen asleep in her chair.

"More secrets?" Maddie asked, glancing up.

"There are no secrets," he replied, then followed Eileen into the hallway.

"What do you need?" she asked when they were alone.

"I was thinking about the accident. Do you know much about it?"

Eileen thought a moment. "The police didn't tell me very much. I know that it had rained earlier that day, so the highway may have been slippery. Jess had driven to Colma for paint and groceries. She'd mentioned to me earlier when she picked up my kids that she might do that. No one knows what caused her to spin out and roll the car, though."

"Did you see the car after the accident?"

She shook her head. "No. The kids were waiting at their schools to be picked up, and when Jess didn't show, my daughter called me. I picked them up and took them to my house. I called the police station because I was worried, and that's when I found out about the accident. I went to the hospital alone that night to check on her."

"I hoped you might know more," Clay said, disappointed.

"Wait." Eileen dug around in her purse, then handed him a business card. "An officer was here that night and gave me this. He can give you more information."

Clay looked at the name of the officer, Darrin Brinkley. "Thanks. I'll call him and see what he knows."

She nodded. "How are the girls doing?"

"Fine, for the most part. Worried about their mom. Trying to get used to me again. It's been tough on them, though," he said.

"Well, I'm here to help if you need me."

Hesitating, he rubbed his hand on the back of his neck. "There is one favor I wanted to ask. Could the girls stay with you for an hour or so tonight? I have somewhere I need to be at seven o'clock."

She studied him carefully. Clay figured she was weighing whether or not it was her business to ask where he was going. Finally, she said, "Why don't you bring them by at six, and they can eat dinner with us?"

"Thanks. That would be perfect."

After Eileen left, Clay walked down the hall a short distance so the girls couldn't overhear. He called the police station and asked for Officer Brinkley. Unfortunately, the officer was on patrol so Clay left his name and number. When he walked back into the room, Maddie stared at him a moment, then returned to her book.

Clay knew he and Maddie had to talk about her anger at some point, but not just yet. His emotions were too raw to start that conversation. He hoped that after his meeting tonight, he'd feel calmer and ready to explain some things to both girls. They deserved an amends from him, and he planned on following through with it soon.

After a couple more hours of painful silence and no change in Jess's condition, he spoke up. "Girls, I have to be somewhere at seven, so I'm dropping you off at the Neilsons' house at six, and you can eat dinner with them. I promise I won't be long."

Maddie's eyes shot up. "I want to stay here with Mom. We stayed later last night."

"I know, Madds. I'm sorry. But we can't tonight. I promise we'll come back tomorrow to see your mom, okay?"

"Where do you have to go? You don't even live around here or know anyone. Are you going to a bar?" Maddie's eyes burned at him, her anger so stark that even Jilly leaned away from her, eyes wide.

Clay's heart pounded in his chest as his nerves unraveled. He stood and stared at Maddie, his words coming out sharper than he'd intended. "Listen, Maddie. I get it. You're angry with me. But I don't have to explain my every move to you. I'm still your father, despite what you think of me. Do you understand?"

Maddie stood too but didn't reply. She shoved her books and notebooks into her backpack and then stormed out of the room. Dropping his head, Clay heaved a big sigh as he forced himself to calm down. When he looked up again, he saw Jilly staring at him, her eyes brimming with tears. He hurried to her and fell to his knees. "I'm sorry, Jilly-bear. I didn't mean to scare you."

She swiped at the tears that had fallen on her cheeks. "It's okay," she said in her small voice. Picking up her backpack, she brushed past him and sped out the door.

He rubbed his hand over his face, angry now at himself for making Jilly cry. Standing, he walked over to Jess, who lay peacefully in the bed. "I'm trying, Jess. I truly am. But I can't do this without you. Please, don't make me do this without you," he said softly. He kissed her gently on the forehead and left the room.

* * *

The meeting started exactly at seven with eight men and four women sitting on metal chairs in a semicircle. It was a typical church basement, with a false ceiling, fluorescent lights, and dark, durable carpeting. But the walls were painted a soft dove gray, and paintings of flowers and trees hung on the walls, giving the room a tranquil feeling.

"Good evening, everyone," a man said, standing up. He was

tall and squarely built with a deep tan that looked like he worked outdoors. "I'm Alex, and I'm an alcoholic."

"Hi, Alex," everyone said in unison.

"As of today, I've been twelve years and three months sober."

A small murmur of admiration went through the group.

"I'm happy you could all make it here tonight. Welcome to those who are new. As usual, we are here not to judge, but to listen. This is a safe place, and nothing said here should ever leave this room. Now, with that in mind, please feel free to share."

Everyone glanced around the room, waiting for the first person to speak. When no one did, Clay spoke up. "Hi. My name is Clay, and I'm an alcoholic."

"Hi, Clay," everyone echoed.

"I've been sober for one year and ten months, and I'll be the first to admit that it hasn't been easy."

"Welcome to our group, Clay," Alex said.

"Thank you. I was relieved to find a local group here. As you can tell, I'm new to the area. My wife was recently in a terrible car accident, and I came here to be with her and our children. Needless to say, the stress is wearing on me."

Everyone in the room sat silently watching Clay. He figured that would happen. It was a small town, and by now everyone would have heard about Jess's accident. But no one had known that Jess was married. Clay took a deep breath and continued. "I'm sure you've all heard about Jess Connors's accident. I'm her husband."

Alex nodded. "I'm sorry about Jess," he said. "I live next door to you, and our children are friends. We're all praying for her."

Clay looked closer at Alex. Was he Eileen's husband? The other half of Neilson Contracting? He certainly looked the part.

"Thank you," Clay said. "It's been the hardest on my girls,

which makes it stressful for me. Your support is important in helping me stay strong through this horrible time."

Everyone nodded.

"We're happy to help you through this," an older woman with short gray hair said. "I'm sure Alex and a few others wouldn't mind sharing their phone number with you in case you need to talk any time of the day or night."

Alex nodded. "I certainly will, and anyone else that wants to share their number with Clay can give it to him after the meeting."

"Thank you," Clay said. "This means a lot to me."

The meeting continued for another hour as others shared their names and what was going on in their lives, good and bad. Clay felt the compassion of the people in this small group, and it made him feel welcome. He'd been to many AA meetings, and most were great groups, but this one was one of the best he'd attended. He was thankful Coop had found it for him.

After the meeting, a few people hung around for coffee and cookies. A couple of people gave Clay their numbers and encouraged him to call anytime. Alex came up to him after a while and gave him his card.

"Thanks," Clay said. "But Eileen already gave me one. It's good knowing that you live right next door, though."

"Yeah. The girls seemed to be doing okay at dinner tonight," Alex said.

"I'm glad to hear that. Maddie is angry with me, and Jilly . . . well, she's trying her best to make me feel welcome. This has been a strain on us all. I wish Jess would wake up. The girls need her."

Alex studied him a moment. "They need you too. I don't know why you haven't been around, and it's not my business, but if Maddie is angry, then she still feels something for you. Jess's accident is a terrible way to bring you all back together, but it could be a godsend too."

"I don't know, man. I would have preferred coming back when they were all healthy and happy."

"I know," Alex said. "We adore Jess and the girls. She's made herself a part of this community in the short time they've been here. Jess is always a willing volunteer at the school, even though she's been busy remodeling the house. And Eileen thinks the world of her. Jess is happy to watch our kids at the drop of a hat, and they share carpooling."

"I'm glad they're at home here. It's been a tough road for Jess, so she needed a place where she felt welcomed."

Alex chuckled. "Sorry. It's not funny, but my wife sure wasn't a fan of yours yesterday."

"Yeah, I know. I was afraid she was going to call social services on me," Clay said.

"Well, actually, she called the police to check on any restraining orders between you and Jess," Alex said with a grin. "She meant well, I promise. She was only looking out for Jess and the girls."

Clay laughed. "I guess I can't blame her. I looked pretty shabby yesterday, and she'd never heard of me."

"Eileen's a good person, and you couldn't find a more loyal friend in your corner. If she knew you were here tonight, she'd understand you better. I certainly won't say anything to her because the meetings are confidential, but if you let her know you're in AA, she'll give you some slack. After all, she's been putting up with me all these years."

"I don't mind telling her. I don't mind anyone knowing. It's a part of who I am. Thanks for mentioning it. I'll be sure to tell her," Clay said.

"Our group meets every Wednesday night at seven. And if you need help in the meantime, give me or one of the other members a call, okay?" Alex said.

"I will. Thanks."

"Well, I'd better get home."

"I'll be right behind you. I have to pick up the girls."

Alex left and Clay did too. Clay parked at the house and then walked over to get the girls. Alex and Eileen's house wasn't too far away, and he enjoyed the walk in the brisk air.

The AA meeting had helped him refocus on his continued dedication to his sobriety. Whenever he became stressed, he knew he needed the support of his fellow AA members. He depended heavily on Cooper too.

Two years ago when he'd left Jess and the girls to go into rehab for the third time, he'd promised Jess it was the last time. He had to make this one stick. And even though he hadn't found the strength to go back to his family since he'd finished rehab, he had stayed true to his promise. Now, he had to work even harder to hold on to his family as well.

Chapter Six

Eileen answered the door when Clay arrived to pick up the girls. The Neilsons lived in a neat, colonial-style house with white clapboard siding and black trim. It stood straight and tall, just like Eileen, and that thought made Clay chuckle. He asked her if they could talk outside a moment, and she agreed and stepped out onto the porch. "Thank you for watching the girls and having them over for dinner," he said.

"I'm happy to do it. For Jess," she said.

Clay nodded. He heard her loud and clear—Eileen wasn't doing it for him. "I have something I want to share with you. Actually, your husband thought it might be a good idea if I did."

Eileen's brows rose.

"I was at the AA meeting tonight. I'm a recovering alcoholic."

"Oh." Eileen cocked her head and studied him a moment.

"That's the reason I haven't been around. At least, it used to be the reason, and I've dragged it out for almost two years. I didn't abandon my family—I've been supporting them financially all along—but I wasn't sure I'd be able to cope with the daily stress of family life and maintain my sobriety. So I stayed away. I realize now how stupid that was, but I can't change it. I love my wife and my girls. Almost to the point where it hurts. I just couldn't bear the idea of disappointing them again."

It all came out in a rush of words. Clay hadn't meant to bare his soul to this woman, but he did.

Eileen's expression was one of surprise, but Clay saw more in it than that. He thought he actually saw her mind shifting gears as she thought over all he'd said. Her face softened, and a small hint of a smile appeared on her lips.

Feeling self-conscious, he ran a hand through his hair. "I'm sorry. I didn't mean to dump all that on you like that."

"No, no, that's fine," she said. "Actually, I'm glad you did. It all makes sense now. I never asked Jess about her husband, and she never offered the information. I suppose that was because she felt you'd join them someday soon. I was just happy to have her as a neighbor and a friend." She reached out and squeezed his arm kindly. "I'm happy to help with the girls anytime you feel overwhelmed. And they can come here when you need to go to a meeting. Whatever you need, just let me know."

"Thank you," Clay said, relief washing over him. "It means a lot to me that you understand."

"We all have our demons. I completely understand."

He waited outside as she went to get the girls. He felt so much better now that everything was out in the open. Having Eileen on his side through this tough time would make his life easier. But now he had to come clean to the girls too. That was going to be tougher. How do you tell your daughters that you are less than perfect? Didn't every parent want to be perfect in their children's eyes? Although Maddie already had a low opinion of him, so maybe it wouldn't be so hard after all.

The girls came out carrying their backpacks, and the three

of them walked the short distance to the house. No sooner had Clay closed the door behind them than Maddie was already heading up the staircase to get away from him.

"Hey, Maddie? Could you come down here? I want to talk to you and Jilly," he said.

Maddie hesitated a moment before reluctantly turning and coming down the stairs. "What?"

"Let's go into the living room and sit down, okay?"

Dramatically, Maddie dropped her backpack, walked into the living room, and sat heavily on the sofa, crossing her arms. Jilly followed but sat down gently and waited, looking eagerly at her dad. Clay couldn't help but smile. The difference between the sisters' attitudes was night and day.

Clay pulled the desk chair over and sat opposite the girls. His heart was pounding, and he felt himself breaking into a sweat. But he wasn't going to give in to his nerves. He had to be up front and honest with them so that they could begin to rebuild a relationship. He needed to make amends.

"I wanted to talk to you both about where I was tonight. I went to a meeting where people talk about their problems and support each other. It was an AA meeting, or, I should say, Alcoholics Anonymous meeting."

Jilly looked confused, but Maddie sat tight-lipped.

"What's that?" Jilly asked.

"It's a place for people who are alcoholics to come together and help each other maintain their sobriety." Seeing Jilly's brow wrinkle, Clay tried again. "Let me explain—" he started, but Maddie cut him off.

"Dad is a drunk," she told Jilly. "He used to sit in bars and drink too much, then come home and make Mom sad."

Clay's mouth dropped open. He'd figured that Maddie

remembered his drinking to some degree, but it surprised him the harsh way she had said, "Dad is a drunk."

Clearing his throat, he continued. "Yes, Maddie, I used to drink. Used to. But I haven't had a drink in almost two years. It pains me that you remember me that way, but I only have myself to blame."

He took a deep breath to calm his nerves. "In AA, when we've wronged someone, we try to make amends. I know I can't bring back the years I've lost with you two, but I want to try and make it up to you by being here now. I'm sorry, Maddie. I'm sorry, Jilly. I love you both, and I want to try to rebuild our relationships with each other so we can all be a family again."

Maddie stood, her eyes spitting fire. "I don't! And I won't take your apology. You left us and didn't come home, and I won't forgive you for that. Mom is going to wake up, and then you'll be gone again. And that's fine with me."

She ran to the stairs and then turned and glared at him. "I hate you for leaving, and I hate you for coming here now and thinking you can be our dad again. I hate you!"

She grabbed her backpack and ran up the stairs, leaving Clay and Jilly to stare after her. Clay dropped his head into his hands. Why had he thought he could do this? Maddie was right. He didn't deserve to be their father. Apologizing wasn't enough. He had to do so much more to prove to her that he meant every word. He lifted his head and stared right into Jilly's eyes. She was still sitting there, watching him.

"Do you hate me too, Jilly-bear?" he asked softly.

She slowly shook her head.

"Why not?"

Jilly stood and looked at him with sad eyes. "I don't really remember you enough to hate you."

Clay's heart clenched, and tears filled his eyes. "Oh, Jilly-bear. I think that's worse than if you hated me."

Jilly reached out and wrapped her arms around his neck. He pulled her close, hugging her tightly.

"I'm sorry, Dad. Don't be mad. I want to get to know you. I want you to stay. Maddie won't stay angry forever. She'll like you again," Jilly said.

Swallowing hard, he pulled away to look at Jilly. "I'm not mad at you, sweetie. I could never be mad at you. We'll just have to work on getting to know each other again, okay? And I'll keep trying with Maddie too. I promised you earlier today that I wasn't going to leave again, and I meant that. We're going to be a family again. Will you help me?"

Jilly nodded her head.

"Okay." He gave his daughter a soft kiss on the cheek, and together they walked to the stairs. "Good night, Jilly-bear."

"Good night, Daddy."

As he watched her walk up the stairs, Clay vowed he would never leave his children again. No matter what.

* * *

Clay walked into the kitchen for a glass of water. He was so wound up after the emotions of the evening that he knew he wouldn't be able to sleep yet. As he searched through the cupboards for a glass, he noticed that there was a small wine refrigerator installed under the counter, filled with bottles. Jess wasn't much of a drinker, so he figured she had stocked it for the guests. In the past, he'd rarely drunk wine, but tonight those bottles were too much of a temptation. He hurried to find a glass, filled it with water, and put as much distance between himself and those bottles as he could.

Stepping onto the front porch, he sat wearily in one of the rockers. The night was clear, and the air was crisp. He inhaled deeply, taking in the salty air, and listened to the sound of the waves caressing the rocks below. He loved the ocean—always had—and that was where he and Jess had spent most of their time together when they were dating. They'd drive along Highway 1 and stop at little diners to eat. In the evenings they'd walk along the shore, talking about their pasts and hopes for the future. Jess was different from any other girl he'd dated. She was beautiful and fun to be around, but she was also smart and ambitious. He'd admired that because he'd had goals too, and he'd found that the more time he'd spent with her, the more he'd wanted to make their relationship permanent—something he'd never imagined before.

* * *

August 2001

The warm evening breeze kissed their cheeks as Clay and Jess sat on the beach near the Redondo Beach Pier. It was exactly two months to the day since their first date, and from that day on they'd spent every spare minute together. Jess became Clay's groupie, and on nights that she didn't work at the bar, she sat in the audience where his band played and cheered them on. Clay loved her being there. Playing music was important to him, and he was thrilled to share it with her. The other band guys liked her too, treating her like a younger sister. Cooper James, their bass player and Clay's closest friend, adored Jess.

"How'd a guy like Clay ever get a girl like you?" he'd tease her every time he saw her.

"Just lucky, I guess," she'd say with a wink.

Since tonight was special, Clay had taken Jess to a nice restaurant. She'd dressed up for him in a blue Hawaiian-flowered-print sundress and strappy sandals. The blue enhanced her eyes, and her tan shoulders and legs were irresistible. He'd brought along a single red rose, and Jess had smiled wide at him when he handed it to her.

"I didn't know you were such a romantic," she told him. "You surprise me."

"Let's hope I can keep surprising you," he teased.

Now, sitting on the beach as the sky darkened around them, he kissed her like he had on their first date. When their lips parted, he gazed down at her, caressing her cheek.

"I've never felt this way about anyone else," he told her. "You've changed me, you know that?"

She grinned. "How?"

"I promised myself that I wouldn't fall in love until I was a famous musician. But I'm not famous yet, and I've already fallen in love."

"I'm falling in love with you too," Jess said softly. "And believe me, I wasn't looking for a musician." Her eyes sparkled mischievously.

"Let's go somewhere we can be alone."

Jess smiled sweetly. "That would be nice, but where? I live with two nosy roommates, and you do too."

"I know of a little cove down the highway where people rarely go."

"You know all the best places," Jess teased.

They drove south on the curvy coastal road until they came to a quiet spot where they turned off onto a small road that headed down toward the cove. Clay stopped in the parking lot that overlooked the beach and positioned his car so the tailgate faced the ocean. No other cars were there, and the lifeguard shack was locked up for the night. They stepped out of the truck, and he opened the tailgate so they could sit on it and feel the cool breeze off the water. He set out the blanket that he kept in his truck, and they sat on it, snuggling close. By now the stars had filled the sky and twinkled above as the moon left a silver streak across the water.

"It's beautiful here," Jess said. "How did you find this place?"

"Our band played here once for a big birthday bash. We've played in all sorts of crazy places." He reached behind him for the cooler he'd brought along and pulled out two bottles of beer, handing one to Jess.

"What other strange places have you played?" she asked.

"Let's see. We played at a zoo once. The guy had rented out the entire place for a night so he could have a party. The spot where we were set up was a distance from where the animals were, but the loud music still bothered them. The elephants and monkeys joined in, causing quite a commotion."

Jess laughed. "Such a glamorous life you lead."

Clay wrapped his arms around her and kissed her. "Do you know the best place I've ever played?"

"Where?"

"A little bar just down the street from the Redondo Pier. There's a waitress there who wouldn't give me the time of day. I fell madly in love with her."

"Lucky her," she whispered before their lips met again.

They made love, slowly and tenderly, under the stars. Their music was the sound of the waves lapping against the shore, and the glow of the moon was their spotlight as their bodies moved together in sweet harmony.

Chapter Seven

"We need groceries," Maddie blurted out as soon as Clay entered the kitchen the next morning.

Clay was in desperate need of coffee after his restless night. Thinking about the first time he and Jess had made love had only made him worry more about her lying in the hospital in a coma. What if he never had a chance to hold her again? His love for her had never wavered, even while they were apart. He couldn't bear losing her now without being able to tell her again how much he loved her.

"Did you hear me? We need groceries. We're out of almost everything."

He focused on his daughter. She was wide-awake and dressed, standing there staring at him with her arms crossed.

"Okay. We can pick some up on the way home from the hospital tonight," he said. Groceries. Why hadn't he thought that they'd need to buy some? It had only been yesterday that Eileen had dropped off a few necessities, but those wouldn't last forever. Despite his anxiety over Jess's condition, he needed to step up here at home. Things like groceries didn't just appear out of nowhere. The girls needed him to act like a dad. And he was certain that if he did anything wrong, Maddie would let him know immediately.

A grin appeared on his face at that thought.

Maddie sat down at the kitchen island and ate a bowl of cereal while Clay made half a pot of coffee. He saw a notepad on the counter and picked it up along with a pen.

"Should we make a list?" he asked Maddie.

"Cereal, milk, bananas, apples, bread, butter, eggs, and whatever else you're going to need to make dinner some nights," she said matter-of-factly. "Snacks, Kleenex, toilet paper, paper towels. You need to look around to see if we're out of other stuff."

Clay wrote quickly to try to keep up. Dinner? He didn't even know what the girls liked anymore. And other stuff? What other stuff would the girls need? Jess had always taken care of those things when they were together. Living alone these past two years had put Clay out of practice. Taking care of himself was very different from taking care of two young girls. He knew he'd better learn fast.

"Daddy? Can you put my hair in a ponytail?" Jilly came into the kitchen with a brush and a hair band and looked up at him hopefully.

Maddie rolled her eyes. "Of course he can't," she said. "Come here. I'll do it."

A disappointed look crossed Jilly's face, but she turned toward her sister.

"Wait. I can do it," Clay said. "Come over here, sweetie."

"Oh boy. This should be good," Maddie said under her breath.

Jilly walked over to Clay and turned so he could work on her hair. He wrapped the band around his wrist and began carefully brushing her silky hair.

"How high?" he asked.

She pointed to halfway up the back of her head. He easily brushed it up and slipped the band around it several times. "Ta-da! There you go, Jilly-bear."

She turned around and rewarded him with a big smile, then ran out of the room.

"Where'd you learn to do that?" Maddie asked, looking perturbed.

"I used to brush your hair all the time, don't you remember? I did ponytails, braids, and headbands. For a while, when you were about six years old, I was the only person you'd let brush your hair."

Maddie's eyes locked onto him. "And then you left." She walked over and put her bowl in the sink, then left the kitchen.

Clay was blindsided by this and not sure how to respond. Maddie was right—he'd gone to rehab for the first time when she was six. When he came home, it took a little time to get back into her good graces. He'd missed her first piano lesson and the family picnic on the last day of school. He had disappointed her, and it had torn his heart out knowing that. But she forgave him eventually, and they'd been close again. Until the next time he left.

Maddie had lived with a lot of disappointment, all because of him. He'd just have to gain her trust again.

His cell phone rang as he was loading the dishwasher. It was Officer Brinkley, returning his call.

"I'm sorry I didn't get back to you yesterday," the officer said. "I had a long shift."

"That's fine. Thank you for calling. I was wondering about the details of my wife's accident. Jess Connors?"

"Yes. I was the first officer on the scene. We don't have too much information since we haven't been able to speak with your wife. The road was wet that day, and there were no skid marks to indicate she'd hit the brakes. The best we can figure is she swerved to avoid something, and the wet pavement sent the car into a spin and roll."

"There weren't any other cars around? Or witnesses?" Clay asked.

"None that we've been able to find. Unfortunately, the air bags didn't deploy. Her head trauma may be the result of that. Other than that, there's not much to tell. Did you need information for your insurance claim?" Officer Brinkley asked.

Clay hadn't even thought about insurance yet. "I suppose I'll need a report. I'll check with our insurance company. Do you know where the car is now?"

"It's at the impound. You can go look at it and let them know what you want done. It was a total loss. I'm sure an insurance adjuster will want to see it too."

"Thank you for your help, Officer," Clay said.

"You're welcome. How is your wife doing?"

"She's still unconscious. We're hoping she'll wake up soon."

"I'm sorry to hear that," the officer said sincerely. "I'm always in awe of how quickly things can change. One wrong turn of the wheel can alter everything. I hope she'll be okay."

After he hung up, Clay thought about what the officer said. He was right; one minute things can be perfect, the next, disaster.

For a recovering alcoholic like him, one wrong choice could change everything. That one sip of beer, that one drink he was sure he could handle. But then one turned into many. One wrong turn. One wrong choice. He understood the devastation that *one* moment could cause.

Sighing, he turned his thoughts to all he had to do. Luckily, he and Jess still had their insurance together, so he could file the claim for her. That way she would have money for a new car when she woke up.

He was thankful the girls hadn't been in the car during the accident. If anything had happened to all three of them, he wouldn't have been able to deal with that. Jess being in a coma was devastating enough.

He and the girls spent the morning and afternoon sitting with Jess again, but there was no change. Her bruises were shifting in color from the dark purple they were at first to a lighter green as they healed. The cuts on her face and arms were slowly healing. But she continued to sleep, unaware that her family was there. Jilly talked to her mom, but Maddie continued her silence. Clay figured she was still stewing about their morning conversation, so he gave her some space.

In the late afternoon, they said good-bye to Jess and headed to the grocery store nearest their house to load up on supplies. He let the girls buy whatever they wanted. He knew some of their cereal and snack choices weren't healthy, but he would cut them some slack this one time. Their mother was lying in a hospital; a little junk food wasn't going to hurt them.

He made grilled cheese sandwiches and soup for dinner, and afterward Jilly helped him load the dishwasher while Maddie sat at the counter, glancing through a magazine that had come in the mail. It seemed like the idyllic family evening, except Jess wasn't there, leaving them to feel the weight of her absence.

The girls went upstairs, and Clay felt lost. Night had rolled in along with the evening fog, and it was cold and damp outside. He wandered into the living room and spied his guitar case where he'd left it that first night. Pulling the instrument out, he sat on the desk chair. Clay owned several guitars, but this acoustic one was his oldest and favorite. His years of playing had left the wood scratched and worn, but the sound that came from this guitar was as rich as the first day he'd strummed the strings.

After picking and tuning a few strings, he began playing the song that had been teasing his mind all day. It was a sweet love song, one he'd played often and that held his heartstrings.

Jilly walked in so quietly that it startled Clay when he opened his eyes and saw her standing there staring at him.

"Hey, Jilly-bear. I thought you were upstairs."

"What was that song? It was so pretty," she said.

He smiled. "That was your mom's favorite song. It's the one that we had our first dance to at our wedding. It's called 'Colour My World.'"

"Can you keep playing it?"

"Sure."

Clay began the song again, picking out the tune. After the intro, he started singing in his deep, smooth voice. "As time goes on, I realize, just what you mean, to me."

As he sang, Clay remembered the day he and Jess had married, how beautiful she'd looked and how happy he'd been. Tears formed in his eyes, and as he finished, he had to swipe them away with the sleeve of his shirt.

"I thought that song made you happy," Jilly said, looking upset by his tears.

"It does," he assured her. "Sometimes something can make you feel so happy that it makes you cry."

"It's pretty. I like it," she declared.

"I'm glad you do," he said. "It's meant to be played on the piano, though. Then it's really pretty."

"Play something else. Please?" Jilly asked.

He played a little of "Stairway to Heaven" and "Peaceful Easy

Feeling." He loved how Jilly's blue eyes twinkled as he played. They reminded him so much of Jess's, and it warmed his heart to think that they had created this amazing child.

"What kind of music do you like?" Clay asked after he finished playing.

She shrugged. "I like Taylor Swift, and there are a few songs my friends play that I like, but I don't know who sings them."

"I bet you didn't know I met Taylor Swift once," he said with a grin.

Jilly's eyes grew wide. "Really? How?"

"My band played before her in a concert in LA. We were a last-minute replacement for her usual warm-up band. I met her backstage. She was really nice."

"Wow. That is so cool," Jilly said.

Clay looked at the clock and saw it was after nine. "We should get you to bed. I don't want you to be tired tomorrow."

She looked disappointed but nodded, and they walked to the staircase. They both glanced up and saw Maddie sitting on the first landing, daydreaming.

"Hey, Maddie. Why didn't you join us?" Clay asked.

She looked startled when she saw them standing there. Acting as if she'd been caught doing something wrong, she stood quickly and fled up the stairs.

"Maddie? Maddie!" Clay called after her, but a moment later he heard her bedroom door shut.

"I think she was spying on us," Jilly whispered conspiratorially.

He bent down to her level. "I think you're right," he whispered back.

She giggled, and Clay laughed along. As they headed up the stairs, Clay couldn't help but grin. Maddie had been interested enough in what they were doing to sit on the landing and listen.

Maybe next time he could persuade her to join in. That would be nice.

* * *

Over the next few days, nothing changed. Jess continued to sleep as they sat there watching her for any signs of movement. Maddie's hostility toward Clay hadn't changed, either. No matter what he did, it was wrong. Maddie only answered him with single syllables and always looked mad when Jilly paid attention to him. It was all so frustrating, but he used every bit of his patience to ignore her anger. He thought that if he proved he was there to stay, she might soften toward him. At least, he hoped so.

On Sunday evening, as they ate pizza and salad for dinner, he brought up the subject of school.

"I think you both should return to school this week," he said. "If you miss much more, it will be harder to catch up, even with the work Eileen has brought you. I promise we'll visit your mother every day after school."

Maddie's eyes darted up and she glared at him. "I don't want to go to school. I want to be with Mom. What if she wakes up and no one is there? She'll think we don't care."

"Sweetie, I'm sure your mom would want you to go back to your usual routine. She'll understand if we're not there if she wakes up. I'm sure of it," he said gently.

Maddie stood up. "What would you know? You don't know how Mom feels. And what do you mean, *if* she wakes up? She's going to wake up. She has to!"

He regretted his word choice. "Maddie, honey, please calm down. I didn't mean it that way. I meant *when* she wakes up. Of course she's going to. I just want you both to have more to do than sit and worry about your mom every day."

"You don't care what we think at all!" Maddie screamed. "That's why you never came back. And now you want to act like you're our dad again. I hate that you came back, and I hate that you think you can tell us what to do!" She ran out of the room and up the stairs. Clay heard her bedroom door slam closed.

Clay rubbed his hand over his face, trying to remain calm. His heart was pounding, and his nerves were on edge. He didn't know how much more of Maddie's angry outbursts he could take. When he looked up, he saw Jilly staring at him.

"Sorry, Jilly-bear. I hope you aren't mad at me too."

Jilly stood up and walked over to her father. She reached up to him, and Clay thankfully drew her into a hug.

"Don't worry, Dad. Maddie is just like that. Mom says it's because she's almost a teenager."

He chuckled, surprising himself. "I guess you're right."

"I don't mind going to school tomorrow. I'll still think about Mom, but I know she'll understand."

Pulling Jilly close again, he kissed her cheek. "Thanks, sweetie. I don't know what I'd do if you were angry with me too."

Jilly looked up at him. "I missed swimming practice last week. I have it on Monday nights. Can you take me tomorrow night?"

"Of course. I didn't know that you were a swimmer. Are you part of a team?" Clay asked.

Jilly nodded her head. "I've been swimming with the Dolphin team for two years. When I'm ten, I can move up to Sharks. We have two swim meets a year, but when I get older I can go to more."

"Wow, that's great. I can't wait to see you swim."

Jilly went upstairs to finish her schoolwork, and Clay cleaned up the dinner dishes. After that, he called Eileen. He wasn't sure about the girls' school schedules and figured she'd know.

"How are things going with the girls?" Eileen asked.

"Okay. Jilly's a sweetheart. Maddie is still angry. But we're hanging in there," Clay told her.

"Maddie's emotions are probably running all over the place. I have a twelve-year-old girl too. She and Maddie are best friends. So I know how emotional they can be. And this isn't an easy time for Maddie, either. Can I give you some advice?"

"Sure. I need all the help I can get," he said.

"Don't let her run all over you just because you're all having a rough time. She still needs structure and limits. She'll respect you more as a parent if you lay out your expectations for behavior, no matter how mad she is."

"Yeah. I've been giving her some slack because of Jess's condition, but I think you're right. I need to talk to her."

"Jess was really good about that. She's much more easygoing about rules than I am, believe it or not," Eileen chuckled. "But she is tough with them when she has to be. I admire her parenting skills. She's a good mother."

"I know. Jess is amazing," Clay said, thankful for Eileen's kind words.

Eileen offered to drive the girls to and from school for the time being so that he could spend mornings at the hospital. Clay accepted her offer, relieved that he'd have that time with Jess.

"Thanks, Eileen. You're a lifesaver."

"I'm happy to help. And if you plan on going to the AA meeting on Wednesday, let me know and the girls can eat with us again."

"I'll be going for sure, so thank you." He knew he had to

keep up with his meetings during this difficult time or else he'd be a wreck. After he hung up the phone, he felt a little better about the upcoming week. But now came the difficult part—having a talk with Maddie.

Chapter Eight

Clay knocked on Maddie's bedroom door and waited. From his side he heard music playing—some nondescript pop song—and a television show on low. Jilly came to the door and smiled up at him sweetly.

"Can I talk to your sister alone a moment?" he asked her.

"Okay." Jilly went to watch television in the other room.

Clay glanced inside the bedroom and saw Maddie sitting on her bed, a book in her lap, ignoring him. He took a deep breath, released it, then entered the room.

"Madds. I'd like to talk to you." He walked over and sat down on Jilly's twin bed, only a couple of feet away from Maddie.

Maddie continued staring at her book.

"Maddie. Look at me." When she still didn't, Clay picked up the stereo remote from the nightstand and shut off the music.

"Hey!" she glared at him.

"Good. Now we can talk."

"So talk, then," Maddie said, crossing her arms.

"Listen, sweetie. I get it. You're angry with me and upset about your mom. But we're all in this together. Me, you, and

Jilly. So, if you'd just be even a little cooperative, I'd really appreciate it," he said.

"Why? So it'll make *your* life easier?" she asked.

Clay was taken aback by her question. He should have known she would be difficult. "Yeah, it would. But it would also make things easier on all of us. Your constant anger and fighting isn't solving anything; it's only making things more difficult."

"Fine."

"Maddie . . ."

"I said fine, okay?" she snapped.

Running his hand behind his neck, he closed his eyes a moment to regain his composure. When he finally opened them, he said sternly, "No, it's not okay. You have a right to be mad at me. I left, and I didn't come back for two years. Fine. Yell at me about that. Tell me all the reasons you hate me for that. Believe me, you won't be telling me anything I haven't already told myself over and over again. I'm sorry I didn't come back, Maddie. I never meant not to come back to all of you. But it happened that way, and I have to live with the guilt of it for the rest of my life."

He stopped and saw that Maddie was hugging herself tightly with her crossed arms. He could see she was holding back tears.

In a gentler voice, he said, "Madds. I'm sorry I disappointed you, but I'm here now, and I'm not leaving. I don't expect you to forgive me right away, or maybe never. But please, can we just get along enough to get through this? Despite what you think, I love you and your sister and your mom so very much. It might take me a lifetime to prove it to you, and I'm willing to try for as long as it takes. But you have to give in a little too. You don't have to like me, but will you please talk to me politely like you would any other adult and try to drop the attitude at least some of the time?"

A lone tear trickled down her cheek, and she swiped it away angrily.

"Is it a deal, Madds?" Clay asked.

Maddie nodded but didn't say a word.

"Thank you," he said.

He took a moment to let it sink in that a truce had finally begun. Maddie was still staring at the wall ahead of her with her jaw set tight. Clay took another calming breath before continuing.

"Now don't get upset, but I'm afraid we won't be able to go see your mom after school tomorrow. Jilly told me she has swimming practice tomorrow night, and I think she should go. But I'm going to need your help with this. I've never been to one, and I'm not sure what I'm supposed to do. Will you help me? I promise we'll go visit your mom on Tuesday for sure."

Her eyes gave away the anger rolling inside her as she processed the change to their plans. But after a moment of turmoil, her face relaxed a bit.

"Jilly needs help with her hair after swimming, and you won't be able to go into the girls' locker room. I'll do it, if you want me to," she said.

"Thank you," he said, relieved.

She looked up at him. "You promise we'll go to the hospital Tuesday after school?"

Clay nodded. "Yes. And any other night that there isn't something going on."

"Okay."

"Thanks, Maddie. I appreciate it." He stood and headed for the door.

"I'm doing this to help Mom, not you," Maddie said.

Clay stood in the doorway but didn't turn around. He knew

that Maddie was just trying to save face, but he'd take her cooperation any way he could get it.

"I understand. Good night, Madds," he said, then walked out of the room.

* * *

After saying good night to Jilly, Clay went downstairs, made sure the house was locked up for the night, and then dropped onto his bed. It had been another long, emotionally exhausting day. If he were still drinking, he'd be on his fifth or sixth beer by now.

The fact that he was even thinking of beer made him cringe. Alcohol was what had caused all the problems between him and his family to begin with. Slipping back into drinking was not even an option if he wanted his family back. But staying sober was a battle every day. And the tension of the past few days was wearing on him.

He thought about how stubborn and strong-willed Maddie was. As maddening as her behavior could be, he couldn't help but smile. She was his daughter through and through and had Jess's strong determination in her as well. But it would be nice if all of Maddie's stubbornness wasn't directed at him.

As he stretched out on the bed, his thoughts turned to Jess and her battle right now. He prayed that her own strong nature would fight and bring her home to him. Because more than ever, he realized that it wasn't a home without Jess.

* * *

August 2002

Clay and Jess lay snuggled together on his bed, happy and satiated after making love. In the year since they'd been together, his career as a studio musician had flourished, and he was slowly making a name for himself as a talented lead guitarist. His guitar playing could be heard on several popular country and rock albums, and his band had also opened for several of those artists in concert. Clay's growing work schedule had allowed him to finally rent his own apartment, where he and Jess could have the privacy they both craved. She was still working at the bar in Redondo but finally had enough money to start pastry school in September. Their dreams were coming true, but Clay had one more dream he wanted to fulfill.

"If you had a baby girl, what would you name her?" he asked, propping himself up on one elbow and looking down at Jess. Her hair was tousled, and she wore a serene smile on her face. He loved when she looked that way.

"Are you trying to tell me something?" Jess asked. "Are you pregnant?"

Clay laughed. "Smart-ass. No, I was just wondering what you'd name a daughter if you had one."

"Madison. But her nickname would be Maddie."

"Wow. You didn't even hesitate," he said. "Why Madison?"

She looked thoughtful. "I heard that name once—in a movie or something—and thought it sounded strong and confident. I like that. A girl named Madison would stand up for herself and not be stepped on by others. A girl needs to be strong in this world to survive."

"You're a pretty tough cookie when you want to be too."

She gave him a sly smile. "I know."

"Madison Connors. Maddie Connors. Yeah, I like that," he said.

Her eyebrows rose. "And what makes you think she'll have the last name Connors?"

Clay reached over to the nightstand, pulled a small box out of the drawer, and handed it to Jess. "Because I'm hoping you'll agree to have that last name."

She sat up and looked at the box in her hands.

"Open it," he said softly.

She did, and gasped when she saw the diamond solitaire ring.

"I love you, Jess, more than anything in this world. I want to spend the rest of my life with you. Marry me?"

Tears filled her eyes. "Yes. A hundred times yes." She reached up and wrapped her arms around his neck, holding him tightly. "I love you, Clay."

When she pulled away, he reached for her hand and slipped the ring on it. "You can't back out now. You're wearing my ring, and you're in my bed."

She laughed. "You're stuck with me now."

"Forever," he said, pulling her into his arms and kissing her. He had no idea at the time how difficult forever could be.

* * *

Present

The next day Clay got up early to see the girls off to school, but they really didn't need his help. They had their routine down pat—thanks to their mother—and they were up, dressed, and had eaten by the time he entered the kitchen.

"You girls sure are efficient," he said. "Jilly? Did you do your own ponytail?"

She shook her head. "Maddie did it for me. She helped me pick out my clothes too."

He glanced at Maddie, who was busy putting books into her backpack. "That was nice of you to do for your sister, Madds," he said.

Maddie shrugged. "It's no big deal."

To Clay, however, it was a big deal. Maddie was a good big sister.

A horn honked outside, and the girls ran to the front door.

"Bye, Dad," Jilly said quickly before following Maddie to Eileen's car.

"Bye, Jilly-bear," he said from the doorway. He waved to Eileen and watched as she headed down the driveway.

After they left, he called the insurance company to file an accident report. After what seemed like forever on the phone, he got into his car and drove to the hospital. There had been no change in Jess's condition overnight, which was both a frustration and a relief. He had hoped there'd been some new sign that she would wake up. The doctor once again told him that the chance of her waking up was good. Yet she slept on.

Clay sat beside Jess's bed, held her hand, and talked of only positive things. "Maddie and Jilly are both at school today, and I'm taking Jilly to swimming practice tonight. Maddie said she'd help Jilly with her hair after practice. She's so grown-up, Jess. Maddie is the strong, confident girl you wanted her to be. You named her well."

He couldn't tell Jess how much Maddie hated him, or how difficult everything had been. If she could hear him, he didn't want her to worry. Jess needed all her energy to heal and come back to them.

Clay reluctantly left in the afternoon so that he'd be there when the girls came home from school. Traffic was lighter than he'd anticipated, and he made it home before the girls. Feeling wound up, he went down the steep steps to the beach and walked along the sandy shore.

The wind whipped his hair, and water stained his boots, but he didn't care. It felt good to walk off his anxiety. A few years ago, after his second stint in rehab, he'd taken up running as a way to calm his nerves. It had worked for a while. He had run every morning; between that and the AA meetings, he'd kept alcohol at bay. But then he went on the road with an up-and-coming band to fill in as their lead guitar player for six weeks, and everything had gone to hell.

He came to a pile of boulders near the water's edge and sat, staring off into the horizon. It was a wonder either girl spoke to him at all. How betrayed they must feel that their own father chose alcohol over them. How do you explain to a child that the lure of alcohol was so strong it made him choose unwisely? It was a thirst he fought every day, sometimes every minute of the day, for something that could ruin his life. He was supposed to love them more than anything else—and he did—yet he failed them every time he gave in to that thirst. Maddie didn't need to tell him how much she hated him, because he already hated himself for disappointing her and Jilly.

"And Jess," he said to the empty beach. "I've disappointed the woman I promised to love forever."

A great sigh escaped Clay. He couldn't change the past, but he could work hard at making a better future.

"Grant me the serenity to accept the things I cannot change, courage to change the things I can, and wisdom to know the difference." Those were more than just words to Clay; they were the words that had helped him make it through two years sober.

He could do this.

Looking at his phone, he realized he'd been at the beach too long. He headed back to the house. As he approached the front door, he hesitated. From inside, someone was playing the piano, and he also heard the strings of a violin. As he listened to the tune being played, he recognized it. It was his and Jess's song, "Colour My World."

Quietly opening the door, he stepped into the entryway. He glanced into the living room and saw Maddie sitting at the piano, slowly picking out the notes of the song. Standing beside her was a slender girl with long brown hair, holding a violin in one hand and a bow in the other. The girl tucked her violin under her chin and tried playing the notes that Maddie was showing her. Then they both played a few lines together. It was a bit stilted, as learning any new song can be, but it was music to Clay's ears.

Maddie does have my ear for music. Look at her!

His heart swelled with pride as he watched his daughter continue to pick out a few more notes and teach them to the girl.

Movement on the left side of the room caught his eye, and he saw Jilly sitting on the sofa, swinging her legs, which didn't quite touch the floor. He raised his finger to his lips so she wouldn't speak, but Maddie saw the movement and looked up. Her expression changed from surprise to anger. She closed the lid over the piano keys.

"We're done for today," she announced to the girl.

Disappointed, Clay stepped into the room. "Please don't stop on my account. I'd love to hear more."

Maddie stood. "No." She turned to the girl who was staring at Clay. "We'll do more tomorrow at school, Emma. Come on. I'll walk you home."

Emma nodded and tucked her instrument into its case. She

turned and smiled up at Clay. "Hi."

"Hi, Emma," Clay said. "Are you Eileen and Alex's daughter?"

"Yeah," she said.

Maddie scowled and tugged on her friend's arm. "Come on."

"Maddie and Emma were picked to play a duet at the orchestra concert," Jilly said, running over to her dad.

Maddie turned and glared at Jilly from the doorway. "That's not your news to tell," she scolded.

Jilly's excitement waned. "Sorry."

Clay curled a comforting arm around Jilly's shoulder. "That's wonderful, girls. Congratulations."

Emma beamed at him. "Thanks."

"Let's go," Maddie said, nearly pulling Emma outside.

Before the door shut, Clay heard Emma say quietly, "But your dad's so nice. And cute."

Clay chuckled, then turned to Jilly. "Don't mind Maddie. I'm glad you told me about the duet. Is that the song they're going to play?"

She nodded. "I think so. Maddie asked me what song you played the other night, then looked for the sheet music online. She only got one page of it for free. But that was all she needed. She usually sounds out songs anyway."

"She's very talented," he said.

"Yep. That's what her music teacher always tells Mom."

"Well, we all have our talents. I can't wait to watch you at swimming tonight," Clay said.

She beamed at him.

"Let's make dinner," he said. "You want to help?"

"Sure!" She skipped all the way to the kitchen with Clay right behind her.

* * *

Clay sat on the bleachers at the middle school pool and watched Jilly attentively as she swam laps through the water. She moved with the ease of a fish. Clay had never been interested in sports, so it was fun watching one of his children do so well.

"She's really good, isn't she?" he said to Maddie, who was sitting on the bench behind him and a short distance away with a math book in her lap. She glanced up from the sheet she was working on.

"Yeah. But I already *knew* that, because I watch her all the time."

He ignored her tone. "I'm glad I get to watch her tonight. And I appreciate you helping."

"Yeah, whatever."

Clay scooched over a little closer to Maddie. "I really enjoyed listening to you play piano today too. I wish you'd play a few songs for me. You're very talented."

She shrugged. "It's not a big deal."

"I think it is," he said. "Maybe I can help you work on that song. I know it by heart."

Her eyes darted up at him. "No *thank you*. I'll do it myself." Then she returned to her math homework.

Clay sighed and returned his attention to Jilly in the pool. Maddie was one tough cookie, that was for sure. But eventually, he'd get through to her. At least, he hoped he would.

Chapter Nine

Clay spent Tuesday morning by Jess's side and then picked up the girls at home after school and made the trip back to the hospital. It had rained that day, and the dark, wet pavement glistened in the headlights, reminding them all of the day Jess's car had rolled over.

"Don't drive too fast, Daddy," Jilly said from the back seat.

Clay looked in the rearview mirror and saw that her eyes were as big as saucers as she stared at the road. He understood her fear.

"I won't, Honey Bear," he assured her. "I'll be very careful."

He glanced at Maddie, sitting in the seat next to him. She was also staring at the wet pavement.

"Mom had driven this road a million times in the rain and fog, and nothing had ever happened before. How could she have rolled it that day?" Maddie turned to him. "Did anyone tell you how it happened?"

He shook his head.

"You just don't want to tell us," Maddie accused.

"No, Madds. I'd tell you if I knew, but only your mom knows

what happened. The officer at the scene thought she might have swerved to avoid hitting something, but it's just a guess. I wish I knew too."

Maddie turned away. "I guess it doesn't matter. But I'll always think of Mom's accident every time we pass that spot."

"Me too," Jilly said sadly.

Me too, Clay thought.

Jess's condition hadn't changed. Maddie moved two chairs beside the bed so she and Jilly could sit near their mom. Jilly had no words tonight. She sat quietly, studying her mother. Clay watched her from the other side of the bed and wondered what she was thinking. He didn't want to intrude on her thoughts by asking her, though. So they all sat there quietly with the sound of the heart monitor echoing in their ears.

They ate dinner in the hospital cafeteria that night and headed home later that evening. As they rode in the dark car, Jilly spoke up in a small voice from the backseat.

"Mom is going to wake up, isn't she?"

A chill ran down Clay's spine. How could he answer such a sad question honestly without breaking his daughter's heart? There was no guarantee that Jess would wake up, no matter how much he wanted her to. Before he could reply, though, Maddie jumped in.

"Of course Mom is going to wake up. Don't ask stupid questions."

"Maddie . . . ," he warned. "Jilly, sweetie, the doctor said that it's not unusual to be in a coma after a head trauma like your mother experienced. It could be a week, or even five weeks. We just have to be patient."

Maddie crossed her arms and glared at her father but remained silent.

"I'll keep believing, then," Jilly said. "I really want Mom to wake up."

"Me too, sweetie," He said softly. "Me too."

The next evening, Clay attended the AA meeting in the church basement. Maddie had been upset that they weren't going to visit her mother that night, but Clay didn't cave. He explained how important these meetings were to his sobriety, although he knew his words were falling on deaf ears. But it didn't matter; he needed these meetings to get him through the stress and anxiety he was feeling. Without them, he didn't trust that he wouldn't give in to the thirst that plagued him.

"Hey, Clay. Glad you could make it," Alex said as Clay entered the room. Other people waved and said hello.

"Wouldn't miss it," Clay said. "It's thanks to Eileen that I can come. Having the girls over for dinner is a big help to me."

"She's happy to do it. You and she may have had a rocky start, but she's rooting for you now. I hear that Maddie is giving you a hard time, though."

He nodded. "I'm working on that. Hopefully, she'll come around."

After the meeting started and a few others had shared stories about their week, Clay spoke up.

"Hi. I'm Clay, and I'm an alcoholic."

"Hi, Clay," the others said.

"It's been a tough week," he said. "As you all know, my wife was in an accident, and she's still in a coma. It's hard watching her lay there, day after day, not knowing if she's going to wake up. The doctor says we should be patient, but it's not easy. It's especially difficult watching my daughters worry about their mother. My youngest is trying to be brave, and it's so heartbreaking to watch. And my oldest is using her anger with me as a way to hide how frightened she is for her mother. I'm an emotional wreck at the end of each day, and if I didn't have these meetings to vent, I'm not sure if I'd be able to maintain my sobriety."

There were murmurs in the room as others nodded, understanding how frustration can push someone toward alcohol.

"Is there anything we can do as a community to help?" Alex asked. "People around here are always willing to lend a hand."

"I appreciate that," Clay said. "I don't know if anyone can do anything right now, but maybe later. It's been an emotional rollercoaster for me, coming home under these circumstances."

The older woman who'd offered her help at the last meeting spoke up. "Hi, Clay. I'm Corrine. Can I ask a personal question? Why were you away so long? You said you've been sober for two years."

Hesitating, he ran a hand through his hair. He'd figured people would be curious since no one had known Jess was married. But if he couldn't trust telling his fellow AA members his story, then who could he trust?

"That's why I'm having such a hard time with my oldest daughter. I went to rehab for the third time two years ago. It was my last shot to make things right with my family. Jess moved up here to work on the house and start a B&B, and I had always intended on coming up here too, at least part-time since my work is in LA. But after I got out of rehab, the days went by quickly. Then months. Then years. I wasn't sure I could handle the stress of family and expectations right away. Then I was afraid that if I couldn't handle it, I'd lose them forever. Unfortunately, I did a lot of damage by not coming home."

The woman nodded. "I understand. We've all damaged relationships in one way or another. But you're here now, and that's important."

A man who looked like he was in his thirties, with a sleeve of tats on his arm and multiple piercings, spoke up. "I'm Trevor. Any time of the day or night, you can call if you feel like you're losing it, man. I know the pressure you're under. I have two kids too, and I haven't been the best husband or father, but I keep trying. I'd be happy to help."

"Thanks, Trevor. I appreciate it."

As others shared their stories, Clay felt grateful for being there. Everyone seemed sincere in their wish to help, and that made him feel stronger. They ended their meeting with the Serenity Prayer, and Clay took those words to heart. He needed to take things one day at a time and not try to control everything. That was the only way he was going to get through this ordeal.

His cell phone rang on his way home. It was his agent, Jeff Goodwin.

"Hey, Jeff. What's up?" he said, putting the call on speaker.

"I was going to ask you the same question. What's happened to you? It's like you fell off the face of the earth."

Clay chuckled. Jeff had been his agent for the past five years, getting Clay the best jobs in the studios and on the road. He wouldn't be where he was professionally if it weren't for Jeff.

"Sorry to worry you. Jess was in an accident, and I'm up here with the girls. Since a week ago, I haven't had a moment to think of anything else."

"Oh, man. That's terrible. How is Jess? Is she okay?"

Clay gave him a short version of what had been going on and heard Jeff whistle softly over the phone.

"Wow. I had no idea. Sorry, Clay. I certainly hope she comes out of it."

"She has to," Clay said. "So, why are you calling?"

"Oh, well, it seems terrible now that I called, but I was told to remind you about the tracks you're supposed to lay down for Chris's album next week. The producer hasn't seen you around the studio lately and is freaking out. They're on a tight schedule."

"Sorry, Jeff, but I can't be there next week. Can't they give me a little more time for a family emergency?" The last thing Clay wanted to worry about right now was work.

"I don't know. He really wanted you for this song. He's even asking about you traveling with the band as his lead guitarist when they go on tour. It's a tremendous opportunity."

"I know," Clay said. "But I need to be here with my girls. I can't just leave them while their mom is in the hospital. They already have trust issues with me. That would prove I didn't care."

"Bring them with," Jeff said.

Clay's brows rose. "Are you serious? Bring them to a studio session?"

"Why not? You've brought Maddie before. A lot of artists have their kids along. It's not going to take more than a few hours to do anyway. Think about it, okay?"

After saying good-bye, Clay thought about what Jeff had suggested. He hated missing out on being on Chris's upcoming album. He was sure there'd be a few hit singles from it, and it was great exposure. The fact that a country star of that caliber wanted him to play on his album was already a compliment. But being here with the girls and Jess was more important than any album. He'd ponder if for a few days and see how Jess was before deciding one way or the other.

When Clay arrived home, the girls, along with Eileen, Emma, and Jerrod, were there. Jilly and Jerrod were playing a game on the dining room table while Maddie and Emma practiced their song in the living room. As soon as Clay entered, though, Maddie stopped playing.

Eileen greeted him in the entryway. "Hope you don't mind us being here. The girls wanted to practice."

"No, it's not a problem," he said. "I wish Maddie would keep playing, though. I'd love to hear them."

Eileen turned back toward the living room. "Girls? Why don't you continue playing?" But Emma was already packing up her violin.

Eileen looked at Clay. "Sorry. It's getting late anyway. We'd better head home." She called to Jerrod that it was time to leave.

"Just a few more minutes?" Jerrod asked, but his mother told him no.

As he and Jilly walked out into the foyer, Eileen introduced her son. "Jerrod and Jilly are in the same class in school."

"Nice to meet you, Jerrod," Clay said.

The young boy smiled up at him and said, "Hi." He had his dad's dark hair and brown eyes and was tall for his age.

"Thanks for watching the girls and giving them dinner again," Clay told Eileen.

"I'm happy to do it. Jess would do it for me if the situation was reversed. They are welcome every Wednesday night. Just give me a heads up."

After the Neilsons left, Maddie turned out the light in the living room and headed for the stairs.

"Does anyone want a snack before bed?" Clay asked.

"I do!" Jilly said, raising her hand.

"What about you, Madds?"

"I'm going to bed," she said, one foot on the stairs.

He approached her. "I sure wish you'd let me hear you play."

Maddie shook her head. "No. Then it'll no longer be my

thing. It'll become about you. I play piano because I enjoy it and am good at it, not because you're a musician."

Clay knew she meant those words to hurt him, but he took the high road. "I wouldn't take credit for it, Madds. You're right. You play well because you work at it. That makes me even prouder of you."

Maddie stood there, wrinkling her brow. He guessed she hadn't expected him to agree with her.

"Good night," Maddie said. She ran up the stairs before he could say anything more.

"Snack!" Jilly said, grabbing her father's hand and pulling him toward the kitchen.

Clay chuckled. "Okay, okay." As he went into the kitchen, he grinned. He hoped he'd made a little headway with Maddie tonight. *Baby steps. Tiny, little baby steps.*

* * *

June 30, 2003

Clay and Jess were married on a perfect California day at the little cove where they had made love the very first time. They vowed to love, honor, and cherish each other as they stood in the sand by the water, and their friends and family looked on. She wore a simple strapless gown that hugged her small waist and carried a bouquet of white roses and lavender. The groom looked handsome with his freshly cut hair and sand-colored suit. The sound of the waves caressing the beach was the perfect backdrop for their simple ceremony.

Afterward, they celebrated with a reception in Jess's mother's backyard. Clay's musician friends brought along their instruments and played music into the wee hours. Jess's mother, Karen, did as much as she could for them on her limited salary as a secretary. Jess's grandmother, Mavis, also came to the wedding. Her grandfather, Earl, had just died in March, so it had been a difficult few months for Mavis. But she said she wouldn't miss being there for her only granddaughter's wedding.

Jess had finished her first year of pastry school and was planning on going for the second year that fall. A few of her fellow students came to the reception. Two had volunteered to make the wedding cake, and others brought an array of delicious desserts like crème brûlée, cherry tarts, and chocolate truffles. It made the small reception seem like a lavish event, with live music and gourmet desserts, and everyone had a wonderful time.

That night, after all the celebrating was over, Clay and Jess lay in each other arms in bed, sharing their dreams for the future. They felt warm and tipsy from all the champagne they'd consumed at the party. His career had continued to thrive, and in a year, she would be able to apply to upscale restaurants as a pastry chef. They had the world by the tail and were content with what they'd accomplished and what the future held.

"Maybe a little Madison will be in our future," he whispered into her ear.

"Goodness! Let's make sure this marriage works before we start thinking of children."

"What?" Clay sat up in bed, startled. "You're not already thinking of leaving me?"

She laughed warmly. "I'm just kidding, silly. I don't want you to think I'm a sure thing, though. That way you'll always want to come back to me no matter how many roadies try to lure you away."

Clay dropped down on the bed again. "You're not getting rid

of me, lady. I always want to be your sure thing." He kissed her neck, making her giggle.

"That's good to hear," she said softly. "No matter how far away you go, no matter for how long, you'll always come back to me."

"Always," he whispered, taking her into his arms.

* * *

Present

Clay sat on the front porch, thinking back to their wedding and the promises they'd made. He'd meant every word the day he promised to be with Jess, in sickness and in health, until death do us part. Yet somehow he'd managed to make a mess of things without meaning to. His drinking had started slow, a beer or two at home, a few drinks during a studio session, a few more while on the road with a band. And then he'd go home to Jess, and the drinking wouldn't stop. Jess noticed a change in him, but he didn't. He felt he was just having fun, just enjoying a few beers with friends. But when need replaced fun, even he noticed he wasn't quite the same person.

He thought about his father, Bruce, who'd died when Clay was nineteen. His mother had died years before, leaving his father to raise him. Bruce hadn't been a bad guy, just a tough one whose motto was "Work hard and drink harder." He'd worked on the docks as a longshoreman since he was seventeen, and he was proud of it. But as the years went on, his drinking outweighed everything else. It was the booze that eventually caused him to wither away and die.

Clay and his dad hadn't gotten along very well, especially

when Clay started playing guitar to make a living right out of high school. His dad had wanted to get him a "man's job" down on the docks, but that wasn't for Clay. He'd been playing the guitar since he was eight years old, when his dad's friend had given him a beat-up guitar. It was in his blood, as much as being a longshoreman was in his father's. Clay had also never subscribed to his father's "Drink hard" motto, so it was as much a surprise to him as it was to others when alcohol became his undoing.

No matter how far away you go, no matter for how long, you'll always come back to me. Jess's words to him on that night long ago replayed in his mind as if she'd just said them yesterday.

"I did finally come back to you," Clay said into the quiet night. "I only pray I didn't come back too late."

With a heavy sigh, he headed inside the house and to bed.

Chapter Ten

The next morning, Clay's cell phone rang right after the girls left for school. He glanced at it, and panic seized him. The hospital was calling.

"Hello?" he answered, already running out the door to his car.

"Mr. Connors?"

"Yes."

"This is Dr. Bradbury. I'm sorry to have to call you like this, but your wife's condition has changed."

Clay went still. "Is she all right?"

"She had a seizure this morning. It caused other complications. She's having an CT scan as we speak to determine if there has been any damage."

"Damage? What do you mean?" Clay asked.

"I'm not saying that there is any; that's the reason for the CT scan. But after the seizure, your wife stopped breathing on her own. We now have her on a ventilator. The scan is to check if there are any internal injuries that we might have missed the first time. I'm sorry I had to tell you this over the phone. Will you be coming here today as usual?"

"I'm on my way there now."

"Good. We can talk when you get here. By then we'll have the scan results and can discuss our options," Dr. Bradbury said.

"This isn't good, is it, Doctor?"

"It's a setback to be sure. But don't lose hope. We'll know more by the time you get here."

Clay's heart pounded as he hung up and stared at the steering wheel. He had to calm down before he made the long drive to the hospital. Taking a deep breath, he repeated the Serenity Prayer several times before he was able to focus again. Then he put the car in drive.

The forty-five-minute drive was excruciating for him. He forced himself not to speed—an accident was the last thing he needed—but it was hard. Numerous scenarios about Jess's condition ran through his mind. By the time he entered the hospital, his nerves were pulled as tight as strings on a guitar.

Dr. Bradbury was at Jess's door when Clay arrived.

"What did you find out?" he asked anxiously.

"Let's sit a moment," the doctor said, leading him to a small waiting room down the hall. Clay was too agitated to sit, but he forced himself to, just to get the doctor to tell him the news.

"We didn't find anything unusual in the CT scan. Internally, everything looks fine."

"Then why did she stop breathing?"

"I can't give you an answer. I'm sorry. The seizure triggered it, but we don't know why. For the time being, we'll keep her on the ventilator and monitor her progress."

Standing, Clay walked to the other side of the room. He felt helpless and frustrated. "What does this mean? Is this a sign that she won't make it? That there is more wrong with her, and that's why she's in a coma?"

Dr. Bradbury stood and walked over to Clay. "I'm sorry I can't give you any definitive answers. But don't give up hope. This is a setback, but it doesn't mean there isn't a chance she'll come out of the coma."

Clay wanted to believe that Jess would still wake up, but it was getting more difficult to hold on to hope. Dr. Bradbury left after assuring him again that things could turn around. Clay tried to believe that as he headed to Jess's room.

The doctor had warned him it might be difficult to see Jess attached to the ventilator but assured him that she was in no pain. Clay took a deep breath to brace himself, then entered her room. He walked up to the bed, his heart breaking at the sight of Jess lying there hooked up to the machine. A strap ran across her face, securing the tubes that pushed oxygen in and out of her lungs. Even though the machine was quiet, it was disconcerting to see her this way.

Sitting down, he reached for Jess's hand and carefully held it. Tears filled his eyes and slowly slid down his cheeks. He'd been trying so hard to be strong for the girls and not let his emotions rule his actions. He knew if he'd allowed that, he'd have succumbed to drinking again. As long as he believed that Jess was coming back to them, he could control himself. But now, he was losing his inner strength. Was this one more step toward losing her? And if so, how could he and the girls go on without her?

"Jess, please. Please come back to us. I can't do this alone. The girls need you. I need you. I'll do anything if you'll just come back," he whispered to her.

The room's door swished open, startling Clay. He looked up and saw Eileen standing there, a fresh bouquet of flowers in her arms. A look of shock momentarily crossed her face, but just as quickly, she hid it.

"What happened?" she asked, walking closer to the bed.

He stood, wiping the tears from his face. "She had a seizure earlier this morning and stopped breathing on her own."

Staring down at her friend, compassion filled her eyes. "Goodness. What did the doctor say?"

"In a nutshell, they don't know what caused it, and we shouldn't give up."

Clay watched as Eileen took a deep breath and pulled herself up straight as if bracing herself. She looked him in the eye. "Then that's exactly what we'll do. We won't give up. Jess needs our strength now more than ever."

She walked over to the window where a row of flowers in vases sat. "I thought I'd change these out. We want Jess to wake up to pretty flowers, don't we? She said she was going to plant small flower gardens around the house this spring and have plenty in pots around the porch. She loves colorful blooms." Eileen stopped a minute and gazed out the window. "You know, I'm not sure I even know what Jess's favorite flowers are."

"Lavender," Clay said softly. "It's her favorite because she loves the scent."

"Ah, yes. I should have guessed that. She always wears a lavender scent." Eileen busied herself with the flowers, pulling dead ones out and replacing the water. He watched her in amazement. Nothing rattled this woman. She was a rock. He wished he were as strong.

"Are you bringing the girls here tonight?" she asked as she finished up her work.

"I have to, or Maddie will be livid. What do I tell them, though? I'm afraid seeing their mother this way might scare them."

"Tell them the truth," Eileen said gently. "They need to

know. If you sugarcoat it, it will be harder if . . ." She hesitated.

"If it gets worse," Clay finished for her.

Eileen nodded. "I want to think positive, but we always have to prepare, just in case."

He agreed. But knowing how difficult it was for him to see Jess this way, he worried how the girls would react.

Stepping closer to Clay, Eileen touched his arm lightly. "How are you holding up?"

He was surprised by her gentleness. "I'm okay, but this hit me hard. If I didn't have to be strong for the girls, I'm afraid of what I might do."

"Alex and are here for you, any time of the day or night. Please reach out if you need to."

"Thank you. I will."

"Would you like me to come along when you bring the girls tonight?"

"I think I have to do this on my own, but thank you."

"I won't mention this to the girls when I pick them up from school. I'll leave that to you. But don't hesitate to call me if you need to."

"I won't," Clay said. He managed a smile. "Thank you, Eileen. Knowing you and Alex are right next door is a great comfort."

After Eileen had left, Clay sat next to the bed again and gazed down at Jess. Eileen's strength had made him feel stronger. "We're fighting every step of the way, hon. I'm not giving up on you, and you're not giving up, either. You hear me?"

He wished he knew if she could hear him.

* * *

Clay was at home sitting in the living room when the girls ran through the door. He had his guitar on his lap and was strumming a song. Music always calmed him, and today it helped him sort out his thoughts on how to tell the girls about their mom.

"Daddy!" Jilly yelled as she ran into the room, dragging her heavy backpack. "Play me a song!"

Smiling, he set the guitar aside and hugged her. "How was school today?"

"Great! I beat Jerrod in chess, twice!"

"Twice? How wonderful. Was he mad?" Clay asked, amused.

"Nah. Jerrod doesn't care if I beat him in a game. He thinks I'm smarter than he is anyway," she said with an impish grin.

He glanced up and saw Maddie hanging back in the entryway. "Did you have a good day, Madds?"

She shrugged. "It was okay. Are we going to see Mom?"

Clay stiffened involuntarily. "Yes. But I need to talk to you girls before we leave."

Maddie dropped her backpack and walked into the room. "What about?"

"Come sit down," he said, standing up, and for the first time since he'd arrived, Maddie did as she was told without question. He grabbed the desk chair and turned it around to sit on it facing the girls, laying his arms on its back to brace himself.

"Your mother is fine; I want you to know that right up front. But she had a setback this morning." He took a breath as he stared at the girls' faces. They were watching him intently. "She had a seizure early this morning, and it triggered something that caused her to stop breathing. They put her on a ventilator machine. The doctor doesn't know why this happened, and even after a scan of her brain, they couldn't find anything wrong. So for now, she'll be breathing with the help of the ventilator."

Maddie's eyes had grown wide, and Jilly looked confused.

"Is she going to be okay?" Maddie asked, her voice small.

"The doctor says she can still wake up and be fine. That's what we're all hoping for, okay? I needed to tell you this so you won't be frightened when you see her," he said.

"Why?" Jilly asked.

"Sweetie, Mom has tubes running in and out of her for breathing, and it isn't scary looking, but if you didn't know what it was for, it might be upsetting," Clay said. He walked over and knelt in front of the girls. "I'm sorry, girls. It was a shock to me too. But I believe that your mom will come back to us. I want you to believe that too."

Jilly nodded slowly, but Maddie only stared at him, her expression unreadable.

"I want to see her," Maddie said.

He nodded. "Okay. Let's go."

Maddie stood, strode out to the entryway, and picked up her backpack. Jilly slowly slid off the sofa and looked up at her father. He forced a smile and offered her his hand, and together they walked out to the car behind Maddie.

* * *

When the girls saw Jess, their eyes grew wide. Maddie walked over slowly and stared at her mother, but Jilly hung back.

Clay bent down toward Jilly and said gently, "If you're scared, sweetie, you can sit back here for a while."

"I don't want to be scared," Jilly whispered. "I want to be brave for Mom."

"You are brave, sweetie. You're here, and I bet your mom knows you're here. Come over and sit on my lap for a while.

Once you see her close up, you'll get used to it."

Jilly sat with her dad until she grew more comfortable. Maddie, however, just stood there staring at her mother, her expression serious. Clay wished he could get Maddie to open up as easily as Jilly did. It was hard not knowing what she was thinking.

"Are you okay, Madds?" he asked.

She glanced up at him but didn't answer. Finally, she tugged a chair close to her mother's bed and sat down. Then she took out her homework and started working on it.

After a time, Jilly slipped off Clay's lap and tentatively walked over to the bed. She reached over and placed her hand on her mother's arm, then began telling her about her day at school. "I got an A on my spelling test today, Mom. Maddie helped me study my words last night before bed. You know, like you usually do? And tomorrow, we have a math test, but I'm ready for it. Jerrod and I have been using flash cards to practice."

She hesitated a moment, then drew closer and whispered, "I'm not scared of that machine that's helping you breathe. I hope you're not afraid of it, either."

Listening to Jilly melted Clay's heart. She was such a sweet, brave soul. They drove home that night in silence. As they entered the house, Clay asked the girls if he could get them a snack before bed, but both shook their heads and started walking up the stairs. Both girls were halfway up the stairs when suddenly Jilly dropped her backpack, turned, and ran into her father's arms, sobbing.

"I want Mommy to come home," she wailed through her tears. "I want her to wake up and be okay again."

Clay held her tight. "I do too, sweetie. We all do," he said, glancing up the stairs and seeing Maddie staring down at them, clearly on the verge of tears too. He reached out a hand for her to come join them, but she stood her ground.

"Will Mommy come home?" Jilly asked, turning her tear-streaked face up to him. "Please promise me that she will come home."

"Oh, Jilly-bear," he said with a sigh. "I wish I could promise you that, but I can't. We have to believe she'll be fine. No matter how hard things get, we're going to believe."

Jilly cried as he rocked her in his arms. Finally, he lifted her up and carried her up the stairs with Maddie following behind. Her tears had stopped by the time they reached the bedroom, and he set her on the bed.

"Are you okay, Jilly-bear?" he asked tenderly. Nodding, she wiped her face with her hand.

"I'll help her get ready for bed," Maddie offered gently.

Clay turned to her, surprised. "Thank you, Maddie." He bent down and kissed his younger daughter on the cheek. "Will you be okay?"

Jilly nodded. Her eyes were already drooping, exhausted from her tears.

Reluctantly Clay left, but he knew Jilly would fall asleep quickly. Turning at the door, he asked Maddie, "Will you call for me if she needs me tonight?"

Maddie nodded.

In that instant, Clay thought how grown-up she looked. "Good night, girls," he said. "I love you. More than you'll ever know." Then he left the room.

Chapter Eleven

2003–2004

Clay and Jess were happy and enjoying married life in the months following their wedding. Clay earned enough money so Jess could quit her waitressing job and concentrate on school full-time. They lived in his one-bedroom apartment but didn't mind the small space because it was just a quick walk from the beach and not too far of a drive for his work or her school.

Friends often gathered at their apartment. His bandmates and many of the studio musicians were always dropping by for a beer and to strum out a tune or two on their guitars. Jess's pastry classmates would come by so they could practice making one of their latest dessert creations. Most evenings, they'd all end up walking down to one of the nearby pubs for a few beers, dinner, or a game of pool. And on weekends, Clay and his band usually played in small bars around LA, and Jess and her friends would tag along. They were all young and carefree, and there was always a party or music wherever they went.

Jess admitted to Clay, though, that her favorite times were

when everyone went home and they were alone. He felt the same way. They loved taking long walks on the beach on lazy Sunday afternoons and stopping at the pier for a bite to eat before going home and making slow, sweet love long into the night. Those times were the most precious of all to them.

One chilly January night, Clay and Jess were alone, snuggled up under a blanket on the sofa, watching a rerun of the show *Friends*.

"Want a beer?" he asked as a commercial came on.

She gave him a sly smile. "I don't think I should be drinking."

It took him a couple of beats to grasp what she was saying. He stared at her. "Are you . . . ?"

"I'm pregnant."

Clay's mouth dropped open, making Jess laugh. "Are you sure?" he asked.

"The home pregnancy test I took this morning said I was."

"Pregnant," he said, feeling dazed. Jess wasn't on birth control pills because cancer ran rampant in her family, and she was afraid to take them, but they'd always been careful. They'd joked about having a little girl named Madison, but now that might come true.

She sat up, a worried frown creasing her face. "Are you upset? I thought you'd be happy."

"No, I'm not upset. I'm just letting it sink in. I guess I thought we'd wait until we bought a house and were settled."

"Do I need to remind you that you were the one who forgot to buy condoms a few weeks ago?" Jess asked.

Clay broke out laughing. "So this is my fault, huh? Then I'll take the blame," he said, pulling her to him. He kissed her gently on the lips. "I'm happy. I really am. Just think. A little Madison. Or, what if it's a boy? We've never thought about a boy's name."

"Are you sure you're okay? I know we hadn't planned on this yet . . . ," Jess started, but he interrupted her.

"Yes. I'm thrilled. It just took a moment to get over the shock. A little baby. You and me," he smiled wide. "Oh, crap!"

"What?" she asked, alarmed.

"What if the baby looks like me? The poor thing!"

Jess laughed and hugged him. "Don't worry. She or he will be beautiful and talented and smart, and all those things a parent hopes for. She'll have the best of both of us."

His eyebrows rose. "She?"

Jess grinned. "I can always hope."

Months later when Maddie was born, Clay couldn't believe how quickly the little bundle in the pink blanket stole his heart.

* * *

Present

Friday after school, Clay once again drove the girls into the city to visit their mother. He'd been there all day and had spoken with the doctor, who had nothing new to offer, which frustrated him to no end. This was one of the leading trauma centers in the country, yet they couldn't give him any answers on Jess's condition.

Maddie and Jilly seemed less upset seeing their mother hooked up to the ventilator this time. Jilly quietly spoke to her mother about her day at school. She'd told Clay that she believed if she kept talking to her mom, then she might hear her and wake up. He encouraged her to do so. Even if Jess couldn't hear her, it was good for Jilly to feel like she was helping.

Maddie was another story. She sat quietly, doing homework

or reading a book. She had a determined look on her face, like she'd made up her mind about something and was going to do it no matter what. Clay wished he could get her to open up to him about what she was thinking, but no matter how hard he tried, she wouldn't say more than two words to him at a time.

They ate at the hospital cafeteria and then sat a little longer with Jess before saying good night. It was past eight o'clock when they left, and as they reached the edge of the city, Maddie spoke up for the first time all night.

"I want to stop at Home Depot. It's on the way home."

He thought he hadn't heard right. "Home Depot?"

"Yes. I need to pick up a few things."

Clay glanced in the rearview mirror at Jilly and saw the little girl shrug her shoulders. "Okay. Home Depot it is."

They pulled into the parking lot, and Maddie reached into her backpack and grabbed a sheet of paper. Clay and Jilly followed her as she strode determinedly into the store and headed for the paint department.

"Why are we here, Madds?" he asked as she stood at the counter waiting for someone to come help her.

Her stance was ramrod straight as she looked her father in the eye. "I'm going to buy the paint Mom wanted and finish the last two bedrooms."

"Why?" Clay asked, still confused.

"Because I'm going to paint them. Mom can't finish getting the house ready for guests, so I will. We have people booked for Memorial Day weekend. I'm not going to leave all this work for Mom to do when she wakes up."

A young man wearing an orange apron came over, and Maddie told him the paint colors she needed. Skylark blue, butter yellow, pearl white, and dreamy cream. It was all typed neatly on a piece of paper that she held in her hand. Clay guessed that it was a list that Jess had made. Jess was always so organized; it wouldn't surprise him if she'd kept a folder to track the details of the remodel. As the man went off to get cans of neutral paint to mix, Clay pulled Maddie aside.

"Honey, I think it's wonderful that you want to help your mom get the house ready, but under the circumstances, don't you think we should cancel the bookings and wait to see how your mother is doing?"

Maddie set her lips into a thin line as her eyes flashed at him. "No! Mom was determined to open on Memorial Day weekend, and I'm going to make sure it happens. All that's left are the two bedrooms and some touch-ups outside and planting flowers around the yard and in pots for the porch. It's all in Mom's note-book. I can do that for her."

Clay stood there feeling uncertain about what to do. He didn't want to upset Maddie, but he wasn't sure he should encourage her, either. "Maddie, even if your mom wakes up in the next week or so, I'm sure it'll take her a while to get back to her old self. Running a B&B while recuperating isn't a good idea."

"*If* Mom wakes up?" Maddie screeched. "Why don't you just say it—you don't think Mom *is* going to wake up! You may not believe she will, but I do. And if everything at the house is perfect, she'll be able to come home and be happy again."

"Madds . . ."

"I'm doing this with or without your help," Maddie insisted. She looked close to tears. He glanced over at Jilly and saw she was also staring at him strangely. He'd told them yesterday that they were all going to believe that Jess would come home, but today he was contradicting that. They thought he'd already given up.

The young man came over with four gallons of neutral paint

and stared at Clay.

"Should I mix the paint?" he asked, obviously having over-heard their arguing. Maddie stared hard at her father, and Jilly looked up at him hopefully.

"Yes. Go ahead," Clay told the man. "It looks like we're going to do some painting."

* * *

Early Saturday morning, Maddie went right to work laying down tarps to cover the carpet in the first bedroom—the blue bedroom—and then taping off the crown molding, window, and door frames, which were to be painted pearl white. By the time Clay had dressed and drunk his coffee, Maddie was already trimming the room with blue paint before rolling the walls. He had to admit: the girl was determined.

"Do you want me to help you in here or start on the yellow room?" he asked.

He'd thought about the situation overnight and had decided that he'd humor the girls and help them ready the house. Even if they had to cancel the guests later on, at least the house would be finished. Maybe it would prove to Maddie that he did still believe Jess would wake up and that he was serious about being a family again.

"I want to do the rooms myself," Maddie said. "But the outside needs touch-ups, and the shed needs painting too. Mom wanted the shed painted the same gray color as the house, with white trim. There's extra paint in the basement."

"Okay," Clay said, resigned to the fact that his daughter was in charge. "Should we plan to leave around one to go visit your mom?"

Maddie nodded as she concentrated on her work.

"What can I do?" Jilly asked excitedly, coming up behind them.

He turned around and lifted her up off her feet, swinging her in circles until she erupted into giggles.

"Why don't you help me outside," he said, setting her down.

"Okay. Let's go!" She took off running down the hallway.

Clay glanced back at Maddie and saw that she'd been watching them. She quickly turned back to her painting when she realized he was looking at her. Clay thought he'd seen something in her eyes, like a yearning to be as carefree as Jilly. He wished he could gain her trust and get through to her that he was here for good. But it was going to take so much longer than he'd first anticipated to convince her.

Clay and Jilly walked around the house, inspecting it for spots to touch up. Maddie had been right. Even though the house had been freshly painted in the last two years, there were places that needed touching up. He noticed that some of the gingerbread trim looked faded and could use a new coat of paint too. He found the paint in the basement along with brushes, then got an old T-shirt from his room for Jilly to wear to protect her clothes.

After brushing the shed down with a broom, he set Jilly to work painting it gray, and then he started working on the house trim. He watched as she made sweeping strokes with her wide brush, first one way and then the other. It made him smile, seeing her having so much fun. He figured he could paint a coat over Jilly's work later.

That afternoon when they visited Jess, Maddie sat beside her mother and told her all about their painting projects and how Jess didn't have to worry about the house being ready.

"I'm following the instructions from your notebook," she

told her mother. "Everything will be exactly as you wanted it. When you come home, you won't have to do a thing."

Clay sat back and listened to his daughter talk, wondering if Jess could hear her. He hoped she could so she would know what a strong, independent girl she'd raised. He was proud of Maddie, despite her animosity toward him. She knew her own mind, and she was determined. He thought those were important traits for a girl. Hopefully, no one could ever sway her to do something she didn't believe in. He wished he'd had those same traits through the years.

Studying Jess, Clay searched for any sign that she could hear Maddie. Her bruises and cuts were healing, and she looked peaceful as she lay there. If it weren't for the ventilator, she'd look fine. But there was no movement, not even a slight twitch of a finger or an eyelid. She was as still as a statue. That fact bothered him, causing him to ponder the thought he'd been trying so hard to hold at bay. What if she stayed like this for months? Or, God forbid, years? The doctor said she could still wake up, and Clay wanted so badly to believe that, but after almost two weeks, he wasn't so sure.

They stopped and ate a late dinner on the way home from the hospital, and by the time they arrived home, the girls were exhausted. Clay said good night as they headed up the stairs. He walked into the dark living room, found his guitar, and sat on the sofa, strumming it softly. It was times like this that dark thoughts plagued him. He wondered if, he'd come back to Jess and the girls sooner that maybe the accident wouldn't have happened. Maybe Jess wouldn't have been so stressed and would not have hurried, as it seemed she did that day. Maybe he would have been with her, driving, and they would have been safe. Maybe. Too many *maybes*.

But thinking like that wasn't going to bring Jess home. All it would do is put more stress on him, maybe even push him down that slippery slope toward drinking again. He stood and carried his guitar to his room, where he hoped playing music would calm him enough to sleep.

* * *

2004–2005

After Maddie was born, their life changed. They bought a cute little bungalow in an older, quiet neighborhood halfway between Redondo Beach and Hollywood. Clay's commute to the studios was manageable, and Jess was close to her mother's home so Karen could see her granddaughter often. As more artists requested Clay to play on their albums, his work schedule increased.

He'd stopped booking his own band on weekends because he wanted to be home with Jess and Maddie. Since his schedule was so erratic—often a recording session could run on for twelve to fourteen hours—Jess had decided not to pursue a position as a pastry chef for now. She wasn't ready to leave the baby with a sitter yet, and she wanted to enjoy time with little Maddie for a while. She knew that when she was ready, she would pursue her career.

Their home, however, was still a spot where their many musician friends stopped by to hang out, jam, and have a few beers. Clay didn't necessarily invite them over; they just gravitated to him and Jess, so there was always plenty of beer in the fridge and often-large deliveries of pizza if Jess didn't have time to cook. Coop was there frequently, as well as other musicians Clay had met, both in the studios and on the road. Most of them were single, but they adored Jess and Maddie.

Sometimes, Maddie fell asleep to their acoustic music as the men played and sang and picked out new tunes to songs they were writing. When she was awake, she'd laugh, squeal, and clap to their songs, keeping rhythm in her baby swing or walker. One or another of the guys would swing her in the air or hold her and dance with her, eliciting delighted giggles from her. Maddie had many "uncles" who adored her, and Jess often told Clay that she felt lucky to have so many good friends who felt like extended family.

There was one rule that Jess did ask Clay to follow: no drinking when he was caring for Maddie alone. If she went shopping or out to lunch with a friend, and Clay was in charge of the baby, she wanted him to be alert and sober. For the most part, he followed the rule. But not always.

"It was only a couple of beers," he'd tell her. "We were just having fun."

"It wouldn't be *fun* if something happened to Maddie," Jess insisted.

"Come on, hon. I'd never put Maddie in any danger. You know that," he assured her. He didn't understand why a beer or two would hurt. It wasn't like he was his father, who'd been drunk every waking minute of the day.

When their daughter was almost a year old, Jess found a weekend job with a restaurant as the assistant pastry chef. She told Clay how excited she was to finally use her schooling and create delicate, delicious desserts. He supported her desire to work, and he took care of Maddie those mornings and afternoons that Jess was at the restaurant. If he had to work too, Karen was always happy to spend time with her granddaughter.

For several months, it seemed as if the arrangement was perfect. Those two days a week, Jess would go to the restaurant by five in the morning and be home by two thirty. Usually, Clay and Maddie would have just come home from the playground, or a few of the guys would be over, playing music while Maddie clapped along. Sometimes, Clay would have a beer or two, nothing over the top, and all was fine. But one afternoon he went too far.

Jess came home one drizzly December day around three in the afternoon to Clay sleeping soundly on the sofa and Maddie screaming in her room. She hurried to check on the baby. Maddie was standing in her crib, her face red and tearstained as if she'd been crying for hours.

"Clay! Wake up!" Jess shook him, but he just lay there, out cold. There were empty beer bottles all around him and even more in the recycling bin.

When she finally woke him, he was groggy.

"What? What's wrong?" he asked, sitting up. His brain was foggy. "Are you home already?"

Jess glared at him as she held Maddie in her arms. "Were you passed out? With our baby in the other room? How could you? You promised you wouldn't drink when you were watching Maddie."

"What's the problem? Maddie's fine. She got up early, right after you left, so I fed and dressed her. Then she was sleepy, so I put her down for a nap. A couple of guys dropped by for a while. I just fell asleep on the sofa."

"No, you passed out on the sofa. Maddie was screaming when I came in. She's been crying longer than a few minutes," Jess told him.

"I'm sorry, hon. I am. I didn't hear her. I was tired. I promise,

I only had a couple of beers," Clay said, but he was lying. He'd had several. It had been a long week, and when the guys dropped by, he'd used it as an excuse to blow off steam. "I'm so sorry, Jess. I promise it won't happen again."

Jess made sure it didn't. She quit her job the next day and stayed home to watch Maddie herself. Clay tried to talk her out of quitting. He assured her he wouldn't do it again. But Jess was angry and wouldn't listen. He hated that she gave up her job because of him. He should have been more reliable. He knew that. What scared him the most, though, was that he'd chosen those beers over the safety of his little girl. He promised Jess he'd do better. He'd prove to her he was dependable and she could go back to her job. At the time, he'd meant it.

Chapter Twelve

Clay and the girls spent Sunday the same as they had Saturday, first working on the house, then driving into the city to see Jess. Maddie was quieter than the day before, only telling her mother that they were still working on the house and that it would be finished soon. Jilly barely said a word. Clay thought that they were all at a loss as to what to say anymore. Without any response or positive change in two weeks, it was getting harder to sound cheerful.

Eileen stopped in and brought Emma and Jerrod along to cheer up the girls. Clay noticed that it helped. The older girls sat and chatted while Jerrod and Jilly opened her notebook and played a few games of hangman. Eileen fidgeted with the flowers, freshening them up. Clay had learned that she wasn't one to sit still—ever. But he appreciated the reassuring presence she brought with her. She spoke with confidence that Jess would come out of her coma any day now, and it revived the girls' faith.

"How do you do it?" Clay asked her quietly, away from the kids.

"Do what?" Eileen asked, looking confused.

"Keep your spirits up after all this time. Continue to believe that all will be fine."

She looked at him seriously. "Because I can't bear to think of the alternative. Can you?"

"No," Clay admitted. "I can't, either."

Eileen suggested they all go out for dinner, and they ended up at a Chinese buffet. The kids were happy to be with their friends, and Clay had to admit it was refreshing to have someone else to talk to besides the girls.

"You're doing a good job with the girls," she said over egg rolls and sweet-and-sour pork. "Maddie says that you're all working on the house, finishing it up for Jess."

He nodded. "It was all Maddie's idea."

"It was a good one," she said with certainty. "And it keeps you busy. Jess will be pleasantly surprised when she wakes up."

Once they were home, Clay bid the girls good night.

"Tomorrow's another long day," he said. "And we have swimming, right?"

"We could skip it and go see Mom," Jilly offered.

"No, sweetie. I think your mom would want you to go to swimming practice. Right, Madds?" Clay looked at his older daughter.

Maddie sighed. "Yes. Mom would want you to go."

"Okay," Jilly said. "Dad?"

"Yes, sweetie?"

"Maybe some time when we visit Mom, you could bring your guitar and sing her that song she likes."

Clay smiled at Jilly. "That's a good idea, hon. Maybe I will."

* * *

Monday morning after the girls had left for school, Clay's phone rang. For an instant, he panicked, praying it wasn't the hospital with more bad news. He was relieved when he saw the call was from Jeff.

"Hi, Jeff. What's up?"

"Hey there, Clay. How's Jess?" Jeff asked.

Clay filled him in on the latest news, and his agent let out a long sigh.

"I'm so sorry about the setback. I hope she pulls through soon."

"Thanks. So, what's up with you?"

"I hate bothering you, but I'm calling again about the job with Chris. His producer is getting anxious. Is there any way you can fly down here for a day or two? His team will pay for it."

Clay paced as he talked to Jeff. With everything going on, he hadn't given any thought on this since Jeff's last call. His agent had booked this a long time ago, and Clay was never one to miss a job. But how could he leave the girls and Jess, even for two days? The girls would be upset with him. And what if something happened to Jess while he was gone?

"I'm not sure I can, Jeff. You know I would if I could, but we're having a difficult time here," he told him.

"I know, and I'm sorry. But what I'm afraid of is that they will hit us with a breach of contract suit if you don't show up. That's how badly they want you. I'd hate for word to get out that you don't honor your contracts. It's a hell of a thing to have to say that to you right now, but there's always the chance. Isn't there a way you could bring the girls along too? You know they can sit in the studio while you're there."

"I'll think of something. When did they want me there?"

"Would next Monday work? You could be in and out in a few hours."

Clay sighed. "Fine. Monday. Capitol Studios, right?"

"Yeah, that's the one. Thanks, Clay. After this one, we'll hold off on any contracts until Jess is better, okay?"

"That would be great. Thanks, Jeff."

He hung up and walked out onto the front porch. The day was cloudy and cool, and he could hear the ocean waves on the beach below. It was quiet and peaceful, but his mood was a mix of emotions. He wished he didn't have to go to LA, even for a day. On the other hand, he did have obligations. Technically, he didn't need the money. He made a good income and had enough for himself and for his family. But he loved playing music, and he'd worked so hard to get to the top of his game. He didn't want to go away right now, but he had to meet his obligations.

Getting in the car, he headed for the highway. He wasn't sure if he should take the girls with him to LA or leave them with Eileen. He knew she wouldn't mind, but he hated the thought of leaving them. What if Jess woke up while they were gone? Or got worse? That scared him most of all.

As he drove, Clay passed several bars and liquor stores. He imagined how it would feel to stop at a bar and have a beer. He could almost feel the cool liquid slipping down his throat, easing away his tension. He knew his triggers, and stress was the worst of them. It would be so easy to give in to his thirst, but he forced himself to drive on. He couldn't let himself stumble. Too many people were depending on him right now. But oh, what he'd give for a long drink of a cold beer.

One day at a time. Today, maybe even one minute at a time.

When he arrived at the hospital, he sat down next to Jess and studied her face. She looked pale and appeared thinner. He knew she was receiving nutrients through a feeding tube, but that hadn't helped to keep weight on her. Jess was a slender woman to begin with, and the last two weeks she'd faded away even more.

How would she look in one more week? Or two? Or ten? What if this went on forever?

He hated watching his beautiful Jess fade away, day after day. There was so much more life for her to live. So much more for her to do. Years and years of Halloween costumes, birthday parties, and Christmas mornings with the girls. Maddie's first boyfriend, Jilly's prom, both girls going off to college. Jess baking and decorating the girls' birthday cakes, and them all decorating for the holidays together. The thought of Jess missing any of it was unbearable for Clay.

"You're coming back to me; do you understand?" he insisted. "You have to come back to me and the girls. I'm here now—you've made your point. It's time for you to wake up!"

But Jess just lay there.

He sat there all morning and into the early afternoon. Nurses came and went. A physical therapist gently worked Jess's arms and legs to keep the muscles limber. Clay fell asleep for a while, sitting in the hard chair with his face propped up on his hand. He dreamt that Jess had woken up and asked him why he was there. He jolted awake, only to find her still lying motionless. Sighing, he rubbed his hand over his face and looked at his phone. It was almost time to go home to the girls.

That's when he saw a slight movement on the blanket. His full attention went to Jess's left hand. It twitched.

His heart jumped. "Jess! Jess, sweetie. Do it again. Move your hand. Please, do it again."

He watched intently, and then he saw her hand twitch again.

"Nurse!" he yelled, running to the door. "Nurse! Come quick."

A tall, dark-haired nurse who worked most weekdays came

hurrying into the room. "What's happened?"

"She moved her hand! Jess moved her hand!"

The nurse went to the bed and made a quick check of Jess's heart rate and breathing. "Everything looks normal. But I'll call the doctor." She left the room.

Sitting down again, Clay stared at Jess. "Come on, sweetie. You can do it again. Please, move your hand. Just a little. That's all I need in order to know you can hear me."

He watched for several minutes, but nothing happened.

"Please," he urged her. "Move for me. I love you so much, Jess. The girls love you and need you. Show me you can hear me. Just a little movement. Anything. Please."

But she didn't move again.

Dr. Bradbury came in a short time later. "I hear you've had some excitement in here," he said, shaking Clay's hand. "Has she moved again?"

"No, she hasn't. But she did earlier. Twice."

The doctor checked Jess's vitals and looked at the machines. "Did anything happen before her hand twitched? Had you been holding it? Or had the heart machine beeped?"

"No, I was getting ready to leave, and I saw her hand twitch."

"You hadn't touched her in any way? A kiss? A rub on the hand? Anything?"

"No. She moved all on her own."

"Had anyone been in here before that? A nurse, or the physical therapist?" Dr. Bradbury asked.

"The physical therapist was in here earlier today. But it's been a couple of hours," Clay told him.

Dr. Bradbury nodded. "That might be it. Sometimes, after a patient's muscles have been worked and rubbed down, it isn't unusual for there to be movement of a hand, arm, or leg. It's just the nerves responding. Or a muscle spasm. I'm sorry if you thought it might mean more."

Clay's heart sank. He'd so wanted it to be a sign that Jess was waking up. "I'm sorry I bothered you. I thought for sure it was a good sign."

"It wasn't any bother. We want to know if you see any sign of improvement. As a matter of fact, I was going to talk to you soon anyway," Dr. Bradbury said. "In the next few days, we're going to test whether your wife can breathe on her own. It's a simple test, and if she doesn't respond, we can restart the machine quickly. It won't cause any damage. I feel that the sooner we can take her off the ventilator, the better."

"Will you let me know when you're going to try? I'd like to be here if it's allowed."

"I will. I don't expect the first time to be a success, so don't be disappointed. We'll lower the assist of the ventilator and, if she is fine, keep her there a few days before we lower it some more. But at least it's a step in the right direction."

"Thank you, Doctor," Clay said, shaking his hand. When he left that afternoon, Clay felt like some progress was being made. Even though Jess hadn't woken up yet, the fact that he saw her move a little made him feel more confident she was healing. And if she could start breathing on her own again, that would be even better. Of course, her waking up would be the best possible thing that could happen.

* * *

That night, after Jilly's swimming practice, Clay told the girls he needed to talk to them. They went into the kitchen and grabbed a snack. Then the girls sat at the island while he stood facing them.

"I didn't want to get you too excited before swimming, but I can tell you now. Today, when I was at the hospital, I saw your mother's hand move—twice."

Maddie's eyes grew wide while Jilly squealed.

"Mommy moved! Does that mean she's okay and will wake up?" Jilly asked, her blue eyes shining.

He grinned. "She's not awake yet, but it's a good sign. The doctor said it was probably a muscle spasm or nerve reaction, but I think she moved because she heard me talking to her."

Maddie's face fell. "The doctor's right. That's all it was. I've read some stuff on coma patients, and they do move and twitch sometimes. People just want to believe they're getting better."

"Well, I'm going to believe that she moved on her own, not as a reflex," he said, giving Jilly a reassuring smile.

"You can believe what you want, but it's not true," Maddie said.

Clay sighed. She was stretching his patience too thin. "Maddie, why do you always have to be so contrary? Can't you believe for the sake of believing?"

"Yeah, why are you always so *contery?*" Jilly said, staring at her sister.

Maddie rolled her eyes. "It's contrary, Baby Sister, and I'm just being rational." She turned to Clay. "No, I don't believe for belief's sake. I only believe what I see. Otherwise, you can be very disappointed."

Clay knew this was directed at him. He waited a beat, then let it go. He had more news for them.

"The other thing I need to tell you both is that I have to go to LA for a couple of days for work. They want me there next Monday, but I should be back here by Tuesday night."

"If you come back," Maddie murmured.

"I said I would, didn't I?" Clay snapped back.

Maddie's green eyes met his gray ones. "You said you'd come back before, and you didn't. Why should I believe you this time?"

"Daddy? Are you coming back?" Jilly asked.

He turned his gaze on his younger daughter and saw the fear in her eyes. It broke his heart to see her doubt him too. He knew he couldn't prove in only two weeks his sincerity about staying, but he wished Maddie would at least try to believe in him.

In that moment, he made his decision.

"Yes, sweetie. I'm coming back," he said to Jilly. "And you can be sure of it because you and Maddie are coming with me."

"What!" Maddie blurted out.

"Really?" Jilly squealed.

"Really," he said, grinning.

Maddie stood up. "I'm not going with you. I'm staying here and working on the bedrooms. Someone needs to be here in case Mom wakes up."

Clay held firm. "No, you're going. There's plenty of time to finish the bedrooms. We're only going to be gone a couple of days."

Maddie crossed her arms. "What about Mom?"

"I'm sure your mom will understand if she wakes up while we're gone. I'll let the nursing staff know how to contact us," he told her.

Shooting him her best glare, Maddie stormed through the kitchen's swinging door with as much dramatic flair as possible. Clay sighed. But when he turned toward his younger daughter, he couldn't help but smile at her beaming face.

"Don't worry, Dad. She'll get over it," Jilly said.

He laughed. Jilly was his saving grace.

Chapter Thirteen

2005–2009

Time flew by for the little family. Clay's career was booming, and he spent many days and nights at studios around LA, as well as on the road playing lead guitar for both up-and-coming and established artists. He felt guilty spending so much time away from home, but he knew that if he didn't grab the opportunities that arose now, his career would suffer later. And Jess constantly assured him she understood. She knew how long he'd worked for this, and didn't want him to stop because of her.

"This is your dream," she told him many times through the years. "I knew that when I married you. I won't be the one to make you give it up."

He assured her that when things calmed down, she'd have her turn too.

"Maybe we could even afford for you to open your own pastry shop," he told her. "Wouldn't that be fun? You could be your own boss."

Jess laughed. "Maybe. Once Maddie's in school, it could be

a possibility."

Because he was gone a lot, Clay gave 100 percent of his time to Jess and Maddie when he was home. He loved going as a family to the beach and building sand castles with Maddie near the water's edge. Other children would join in, and they'd create a grand castle with multiple towers and a deep moat with a bridge. They'd also go to the park in the afternoons so Maddie could swing. She loved being pushed up high and would squeal with delight while Jess warned Clay not to go *too* high. But he couldn't disappoint Maddie, who had inherited his adventurous spirit and loved pushing limits.

When he wasn't home, he missed his family deeply, but music was in his veins. He lived and breathed it, and the thrill of playing soothed his homesickness. It was at the studios and on the road where he'd let loose, drink a few too many, and fall dead asleep the minute his head hit the pillow. It was easy to do with a lot of time on his hands and a bus or studio full of musicians. He thought he was in complete control, though, because he never did drugs, and he slowed his drinking the moment he was home. What he didn't realize was that drinking was as much in his blood as playing music, and becoming addicted was as easy as learning a new song.

When Maddie was three, she became possessive and clingy with Clay. She wanted Daddy by her side constantly and would cry incessantly when he got ready to go to work. At first, he thought it was cute how his daughter wanted only him, but after a while, he felt guilty whenever he left the house. Jess would call him later and assure him that Maddie had calmed down and was happily playing, but it still tugged at his heart. The guiltier he felt, the more he drank.

Jess didn't seem to notice his excessive drinking, or at least never said anything to him. At home, he'd have a beer or two, but he forced himself not to overdo it. But often he'd come home from work still drunk or hungover, and he'd fall into bed to sleep it off. He managed to hide his drinking from Jess for over a year—or so he thought.

Until the night she had to go looking for him.

It was a chilly March night with heavy fog rolling in and dampness all around. Clay had been in the studio for forty-eight hours straight, napping occasionally on a cot and drinking beers in between with the guys. Everyone was in high spirits because they knew they were working on a special album. This artist would be a hit, they all said. And they were lucky to be on his album.

But the long hours and too much alcohol with not enough food caught up with Clay. He'd said good night to the crew and stumbled out to his car. He should have had a studio car drive him home, but in his sleepy, drunken haze, he thought he was fine. Before leaving, he'd texted Jess that he was on his way home. He avoided the freeways and took side roads home, driving through unfamiliar neighborhoods. Clay learned later that three hours after receiving his text, Jess went searching for him. It should have taken him less than an hour to drive home.

She called Coop and two other friends close enough that she dared to call at three in the morning to help her search. A neighbor watched Maddie while Jess drove up and down streets where he might be. She didn't want to call the police yet—she knew he drank at the studios while playing and didn't want a police officer to find him first.

An hour later, Coop called her and said he'd found Clay. She drove to the neighborhood where he'd been found, only a few blocks away from their house. There was his car with the front wheel on the curb, still running.

"He's out of it," Coop told her when she arrived.

Coop helped put her husband into her car and then reparked the car against the curb until they could come pick it up. He followed her home and carried Clay in and laid him on the bed.

The next morning, Clay woke up next to Jess, unsure how he'd gotten home. She rolled over in bed and looked at him sharply. "Don't ever scare me like that again."

When he stared at her, confused, she relayed the story from the night before.

He tried to remember how he'd ended up there. He recalled leaving for home, but the rest was a blank.

"I'm sorry I worried you, hon, but I was so exhausted, I must have fallen asleep."

Shaking her head, Jess looked disappointed. "No, you were drunk. I could smell the beer on you, and we couldn't wake you up. You're lucky a cop didn't find you that way."

He opened his mouth to protest, but she interrupted him. "I know you drink at sessions and when you're on the road, Clay. I'm not stupid. I've been around musicians long enough to know how they behave. But I expected you to be more responsible than that. You have a family. You aren't twenty-one anymore. I expected you to have grown up by now."

"I'm sorry, Jess. I really am. You're right—I should know better. I promise I won't do that anymore."

"What, Clay? Drink? Or get caught?"

He frowned. "You're acting like I get drunk all the time. I'm responsible. I usually only have one or two."

She sighed and got out of bed. "You think I don't know, but I do. I've seen you come home after work too many times looking three sheets to the wind, and it's not from being tired. I haven't said anything, because I know you're under a lot of stress from working too much. But after last night, I can't be quiet anymore. Maddie and I need you. Don't you get that? I don't want anything to happen to you."

He nodded. "I get it."

"No, I don't think you do. We need you, and so will the new baby," Jess said.

Clay's mouth dropped open. "New baby?"

"Yes," she said, giving him a small smile. "We're having another baby."

His eyes lit up, and he jumped out of bed despite his splitting headache. He pulled Jess into his arms and hugged her close. "That's amazing. Another baby. I'm so happy."

Jess pulled back and looked at him. "Are you?"

"Of course! You know I wanted more children." He smiled wide. "Maybe a little sister for Maddie? Or a baby boy. Wouldn't that be incredible?"

Jess's smile grew bigger. "It is incredible. Now you can see why I need you, now more than ever, not to be careless. Please promise me you'll limit your drinking so I don't have to go through another night like last night."

"I will. I promise you, I will. And I'll cut back on playing on the road too. We'll be fine with money from just the studio work. I don't want to miss any more time with you and Maddie and the new baby," he said.

Clay didn't realize that by that point, it was beyond his control to keep his promises.

* * *

Present

The rest of the week went by quickly with no change in Jess's condition. It was disappointing to Clay that she didn't move again. He'd thought it was a sign of her recovering, but now he admitted it was probably what the doctor had said—just a nerve or muscle twitch.

The doctor did try twice to take Jess off the ventilator, but both times were unsuccessful. He told Clay not to be discouraged, though. Whatever was causing her to need assistance with breathing might just take a little more time to heal. They'd continue testing to see if she'd be able to breathe on her own.

He hadn't told the girls about the doctor's tests. He didn't want to give them one more thing to be disappointed about.

Maddie continued to insist that she didn't want to go to LA, but Clay stood his ground. He told her that Eileen would check on Jess every day, and the hospital had his number if there were any changes. So, on Sunday morning, after one last fight, Maddie reluctantly packed a bag and got into the car. Jilly sat in the back seat, eager for the trip, while Maddie sulked in the front. But Clay was hopeful. Maddie had lived the first ten years of her life in the LA area. Maybe going back, even for just a couple of days, would trigger enough happy memories so she didn't remember only the sad ones of him abandoning them. He hoped it might bring them closer.

It was a long six-and-a-half-hour drive with Maddie silent and Jilly full of questions. Clay was surprised that Jilly didn't remember much about living in LA. She had been five years old when she moved north, yet she remembered little.

"I remember going to the beach," Jilly offered. "And playing at a park where they had a lot of swings. I sort of remember my kindergarten school, but not really."

"Maybe you'll remember more when we drive around," he offered.

It was early afternoon when they drove up a quiet street in Redondo Beach and parked in front of a two-story Spanish-style apartment building with a red clay-tiled roof and black wrought-iron rails on the balconies.

"Here we are," Clay said, getting out of the car.

Maddie got out and stared at the building, her brow furrowed. "Where are we? This isn't home."

"This is where I live now," he said. "I have a one-bedroom apartment, which isn't much, but it's nice, and we're only a couple of blocks from the beach and the pier."

"What about our house? Why don't you live there?" Maddie asked.

He stared at her, confused. "I thought you knew. We sold the house to help pay for the expense of remodeling the home you're in now."

"I suppose that was your idea," Maddie accused.

"It was a decision made by both your mother and me," Clay said. He hadn't known that Jess hadn't told them about selling the house. "I'm sorry, honey. I would have said something if I'd thought you didn't know."

Jilly got out of the car and looked around.

"This looks nice, though," she said.

Thank God for Jilly.

They walked inside the building and through a small lobby, then took the stairs up to the second floor. Clay stopped at a door with a gold plate reading 2C on it. He let the girls go in first before shutting the door behind him.

"Home sweet home," he said jokingly, but Maddie wasn't in a jovial mood.

"Not my home," she mumbled.

He chose to ignore her. "I'll change the sheets on the bed so you two can have the bedroom. I can sleep on the sofa."

Maddie looked around with an expression of disdain. There was a good-sized living room–dining room combination and a kitchen in the corner with an island where three stools stood in front. The furniture was used but still nice, and against the living room wall, several guitars stood on stands. On the other side of the room was the door to the bedroom and the bathroom.

"That's the sofa from our old house," Maddie said. "And our dining room table. You took all the furniture."

"Just some of it," Clay said. "Your mom moved the rest of it to the house up north."

Her lips formed a thin line. "Why do you live in such a small place? I thought you were some famous hotshot guitar player. Why didn't you keep the house or get a bigger apartment?"

Clay studied his oldest daughter a moment. Maddie's tone was gnawing at his nerves. Forcing himself to stay calm, he explained. "I do quite well as a musician, but there was no sense in my spending money on a second house or a big apartment when it was just me. The truth is, Madds, I wanted to live as inexpensively as possible so that most of what I earned went to your mother."

She frowned. "What?"

"I've been sending money to your mom all this time. I guess you didn't know that, either. That's how she was able to afford to live there and renovate the house. Where did you think your mom got the money for groceries, clothes, school supplies, and basically everything else? All the money came from me."

Maddie looked stunned. "I . . . I thought Grandma left her money when she died, or Great-Grandma did. Why would you send us money when you wouldn't come and live with us?"

He drew closer. "Because I love you, Madds. And Jilly, and your mom. I wanted to help her turn her grandmother's house into a B&B. She's always been so supportive of my musical career that when she decided this was what she wanted to do, I backed her a hundred percent. I know it seemed like I abandoned you, but I didn't completely. I supported you financially, and your mom and I spoke occasionally. That doesn't make up for me not being around. I understand that, but I never stopped caring for you, Madds. Or you, either, Jilly."

An array of emotions played over Maddie's face. Clay wished he could pull her to him and hug her close, but he was afraid she'd get angrier.

"Why didn't Mom tell us that?" Maddie asked. "I thought she never heard from you."

"I don't know, Madds. Maybe she was afraid you'd be disappointed if you knew we spoke occasionally but that I didn't talk to you. Your mom must have had her reasons, but you have to know that I helped in every way I could," Clay said.

He watched as Maddie swallowed back tears. She turned watery eyes to him.

"Did you think sending money would make up for not being around?"

"Oh, Maddie. No, I didn't think that. But it was my responsibility to make sure you girls and your mom were safe and taken care of. Believe me, Madds, I wanted to come back. I wanted more than anything to see you girls and be your dad again. But I couldn't. I wasn't ready. I was waiting for the right moment when I'd be strong enough. I didn't dare mess up again. I was afraid it would be my last chance."

Maddie stared him straight in the eye. "Tell me the truth. If Mom hadn't had the accident, would you have come home? Ever?"

Clay was startled by her question. He watched as Jilly slowly made her way over next to her sister and looked up at him expectantly.

"Girls, I'm with you now; isn't that all that matters?" Clay asked.

"Would you have come back to us if Mom hadn't had her accident?" Maddie asked again.

He tensed. He could lie, but where would that get him? Maddie would see it in his face.

"Honestly, I don't know," he said.

Maddie's eyes flashed with anger, and Jilly's face fell.

"I was so scared I'd mess up again and lose you all forever that I kept putting it off. I'm sorry. I couldn't stand the idea of disappointing you all again, and in doing so, I became a disappointment anyway."

Maddie turned and walked over to the dining room, her stance rigid. Jilly stared at Clay, clearly trying to understand.

"But you love us, Daddy. Don't you?" she asked pitifully.

Dropping to his knees, he pulled her into his arms.

"I love you more than anything in this world," he said, fighting back tears. "Please believe me, Jilly-bear. I love all of you so much."

Jilly patted his back with her little hands.

"I believe you, Daddy," she said softly.

Clay pulled away from Jilly and wiped his eyes. "Maddie?"

Maddie stood, her back to him. She shook her head slowly as if to say she didn't want to look at him. He respected her wishes.

Clay's nerves were frayed. He needed air. "I have to get something out of the car. I'll be right back."

He strode out of the apartment and down the stairs. Once outside, he grabbed his phone from his pocket and called his friend Coop. He felt he was on the verge of a breakdown. He hadn't expected the day to go sour. He'd wanted this trip to be fun. But he also understood that Maddie and Jilly deserved to know the truth. Unfortunately, the truth wasn't always easy to tell—or hear.

Coop answered cheerfully. "Hey there, Clay. What's up?"

"Hi, Coop. I needed to talk to a friend."

Coop grew serious. "Sure. You know I'm here any time. What's going on?"

Clay told him about the conversation he'd had with the girls. "It was terrible. I felt like the worst person on the planet. I should have lied and said, 'Of course I would have come back.' But I decided I needed to be honest. And it didn't go over well."

"I don't know," Coop said. "It sounds like Jilly understood. And Maddie just needs some time. She's older, and your being gone that long has probably hurt her the most. Give her some space; she'll come around."

Clay wasn't so sure.

"The big question is, how are you doing?" Coop asked. "You're not thinking of going to the closest bar, are you?"

"No, I'm not that far gone yet, but I'm pretty stressed."

"Do you want me to come over? I haven't seen the girls in two years, but maybe I could cheer them up. And you too."

Clay considered his offer. It would be easier if his friend was there as a buffer, but it wouldn't fix things.

"Thanks, but I'd better go it alone. If I'm going to prove to them that I'm serious about being their dad again, then I have to be there for them no matter how bad it gets."

"Okay. But remember, I'm here for you," Coop said.

"We're going to be at Capitol Studios tomorrow. Maybe you could drop by. I'm sure Maddie would love to see you."

"Good idea. Why don't you lighten things up tonight and take the girls for dinner at the pier?"

Clay chuckled. "It's going to take more than the pier to smooth things over with Maddie. She's a tough one. But I'll try it."

He said good-bye to Coop, braced himself, and headed back inside.

Chapter Fourteen

It took some doing, but Clay finally talked Maddie into going for dinner at the pier.

"Can we agree to a truce and enjoy ourselves tonight?" he asked her. "We have to eat anyway, so it might as well be somewhere fun."

Maddie agreed only because Jilly kept saying she wanted to go.

"Have I been on one before?" Jilly asked excitedly as they left the apartment.

Maddie rolled her eyes. "Of course you have. We lived here for years. And there are wharfs and piers up where we live too."

Jilly ignored her sister. "Dad?"

"Yes, you have, sweetie. Maybe you'll remember this one when we get there."

Clay chose to drive even though it wasn't too far of a walk, since it would be dark by the time they headed back. He passed the bar where he and Jess had met, and it made him smile.

"See that business there?" He pointed at it.

"Yes," Jilly said. Maddie stayed silent.

"That's where I first met your mother. She was a waitress, and I was in the band. I tried flirting with her, but she ignored me. I won her over, eventually."

"Yeah, yeah, I've heard this before," Maddie said, crossing her arms. "Mom said she didn't date guys with ponytails so you cut it off, and then she went out with you."

"That's right," Clay said.

"You had a ponytail?" Jilly asked, giggling.

"Sure," Clay said. "I was young and in a band. I thought I was pretty cool."

"Right," Maddie interjected.

"Truce, remember, Madds?" he said.

Maddie let out a long, dramatic sigh.

He parked a little way from the pier, and they walked the short distance. It had been a typical sunny Southern California day, so the pier was filled with beachgoers wearing all manner of dress from bikinis to shorts and tees. Clay watched Jilly stare with wide eyes at the people and shops. She wasn't used to seeing people in various forms of undress because of Northern California's cooler weather.

They went to Charlie's Place for dinner and sat at an outside table. After ordering burgers, fries, and sodas, the three sat back and watched the parade of people pass by.

"Can we go down to the beach after we eat?" Jilly asked, gazing at the long expanse of sandy beach just off the pier.

"You've been on a beach before," Maddie said.

Jilly's excitement faded. "I just wanted to walk on this one."

Clay gave her a warm smile. "Of course we can. For a little while. Then I'll buy you an ice cream. How about that?"

Jilly's face lit up again. "Okay!"

After dinner, they took off their shoes and walked along the shoreline as the waves drifted in. The sand was thick and grainy, but easier to walk on where the surf had pounded it down. Clay and Jilly led the way while Maddie straggled behind, obviously not in the mood for a walk.

"Your mom and I used to come to this beach all the time when we were dating," Clay said, thinking back to the days when they'd sit on the beach in the moonlight and drink a beer or two. Everything had seemed so simple then. Easy. He missed those days, before he'd made everything more complicated.

"Is this where you first kissed Mom?" Jilly asked.

Clay chuckled. "Yes, it is. Right about there." He pointed to the spot where they'd sat on the sand in the moonlight and kissed.

"That's so romantic," Jilly said, her eyes shining.

"Oh please," Maddie grumbled. "It's so corny."

"Was this the beach where you and Mom got married?" Jilly wanted to know.

He shook his head. "No. We were married in a little cove south of here."

Jilly took her father's hand as they walked back to the pier. It warmed his heart. He bought Jilly and himself an ice cream cone on the pier, and they ate while walking along, gazing into the shops. Maddie had declined a cone and trailed behind them. By now it was dark outside, and the pier was aglow with brightly colored lights. It was like a world all its own, and he could tell that Jilly felt the magic of it just as he did.

"Did you have fun?" Clay asked Jilly back at his apartment.

She nodded vigorously. "I love it here. Maybe we can come again."

"Our home is up north with Mom," Maddie said.

"Yeah, but we could come here to see Dad too," Jilly told her.

"We'll figure everything out when the time comes," he said. "I'm sure I'll keep a place down here for when I work, but I'll be living up north with you and your mom most of the time."

"What if Mom doesn't wake up? Then what?" Maddie asked, staring hard at Clay.

Clay tamped down the annoyance rising inside him. "We're not going to think that way, Madds. Your mom is going to wake up."

She shrugged and went into the bathroom to change.

Clay hugged Jilly. "Good night, Jilly-bear. I'm glad you had a good time tonight."

"Good night, Daddy," she whispered into his ear. "Don't mind Maddie. She's always grouchy."

He smiled. "I'm beginning to see that," he whispered back, making Jilly laugh.

Both girls went to bed, and he threw a couple of blankets on the sofa for himself. He'd had fun going to the pier and walking the beach with the girls, despite Maddie's bad mood. He loved sharing his memories of their mother with them. Over the past two years, he'd often walked that strip of beach alone, thinking about how his life had turned out and how much he missed his family.

He thought back to the last conversation he'd had with Jess, just a week before the accident. They spoke about once a month, but in recent weeks, they'd been calling each other more frequently. Jess had called to give him an update on how the renovations were going and how the girls were doing. It had been Jess's idea early on that he not visit or call the girls until he was ready to come back to them.

"I don't want them to get their hopes up and then be disappointed," she'd told him. Clay had understood. He didn't want to hurt them any more than he already had.

"I know you'll come back to us when you're ready," Jess always said when they spoke. "You're getting stronger every day, and you will come back."

Clay was always amazed at how much she believed in him even when he didn't believe in himself.

Three times he'd gone to rehab. Two times he'd failed. Because of that, every time he'd thought he was strong enough to go back to his family, he'd freeze. What if he returned and then started drinking again? What would Jess do then? Would she still believe in him or finally have had enough and divorce him? He couldn't bear to think of that, so he'd put off returning to the family he loved dearly. Maddie had every reason to be angry with him. He had to keep trying to show her he'd changed. He couldn't give up, just as Jess hadn't given up on him.

* * *

They arrived at the famous Capitol Studios tower in Hollywood a little after ten the next morning.

"This is so cool," Jilly said, wide-eyed as she stared at the tower made to look like a stack of records.

"I've been here before," her sister said, acting nonchalant, but she still gazed at it with bright eyes. Clay could tell she was excited to be here too.

"Some of the most famous musicians of all time have recorded here since 1956. The Beach Boys, Rod Stewart, and the Eagles, to name a few," Clay said proudly.

"Who?" Jilly asked.

Clay laughed. "Okay, how about Katy Perry and Sam Smith?"

"Really?" Jilly said. "Wow! Will we meet any of them?"

"No, you won't," Maddie said. "I never met anyone famous here when I was younger."

"Actually, Madds, you once met Don Henley from the Eagles, but you were only five years old then," Clay said.

She shrugged.

Clay laughed. "Boy, if that doesn't impress you, Madds, nothing will."

They headed into the building where they were given security passes to wear, then walked through a maze of hallways until they found the studio where he was to record. When they entered the control room, several people were already there to greet them, including Coop.

"Maddie! Jilly! Do you remember me? Your dad's old friend Coop," he said, coming over to the girls.

Maddie's eyes lit up. "Uncle Coop!" she exclaimed.

He reached down and hugged her. "I knew you wouldn't forget a great-looking guy like me," he teased.

Jilly stood there, looking uncomfortable.

"Oh no. Jilly doesn't remember me," Coop said. "Well that's okay, sweetie. You'll get to know me today. I'm a pretty cool guy." He pulled a bag of gummy bears out of his pocket and handed them to Jilly. Bending down, he whispered loud enough for Clay to hear, "I heard these were your favorite."

Jilly's face broke out into a smile. "Thank you."

"I didn't forget my Madds," Coop said, handing her a bag of red Twizzlers. "Still your favorite, I hope."

"Thanks, Uncle Coop," she said, smiling.

Clay wished he could get Maddie to smile at him that way, but he was pleased that she was happy to see Coop again.

Jeff was there and quickly introduced the producer and crew to Clay.

"Are any of the other musicians coming today?" Clay asked.

"No. It's just you," Tony, the producer, said. "You can record your section, and it'll be added in."

"Sounds good," Clay said.

"Come on, girls. There's a spot in the back corner where we can sit and watch while they work." Coop waved to them to follow him.

"See you girls in a bit," Clay said, carrying his guitar through a door to the sound studio. He was relieved that his friend was here to watch the girls while he worked. He knew Coop would keep them entertained.

Clay entered the studio and headed to the single chair that sat in front of a microphone. A gleaming black grand piano was the only other thing in the room. Clay admired it a moment, thinking how wonderful it would be if Maddie could play it. The producer gave him a pair of headphones so he could hear the music that had already been recorded and play along.

"Chris was thrilled that you could make it. He loves how you play," Tony told him as Clay pulled his guitar from its case.

"I'm excited to play on his album. I hear good things about him."

"I'm so sorry about your wife's situation. Has there been any change?" Tony asked, looking concerned.

"She's still in a coma, but we're keeping a positive attitude that she'll wake up any day," Clay told him.

"Well, Chris said that if he could do anything to help, let him know. And me too. Anything at all."

Clay thanked him. It was a nice gesture, considering he barely knew them.

The soundman got into place and cued Clay when the music was to begin. Clay started strumming his guitar along with the music on the headphones. The girls sat quietly with Coop even though talking was allowed in the sound booth. From time to time, Clay would look up and catch Maddie's or Jilly's eye and wink or smile. He saw how absorbed Maddie was in the music.

She's a true musician. She's more like me than she wants to admit.

Clay played for hours as he tried different licks that would fit in with the songs. Coop took the girls on an unofficial tour of the building to kill time, and at lunchtime he took them to a restaurant across the street for burgers. It was after five o'clock by the time Clay finished recording, and even though he enjoyed it, he was relieved to be done. Now he could put work on the back burner for a while and focus on Jess and the girls.

Clay came into the control room, and the soundman played back some of what they'd recorded for him and the girls to hear. All the other instruments were combined along with his guitar playing.

"Wow! Did you do all that?" Jilly asked.

He laughed.

"Just a part of it," he told her. "They mixed what I did today along with what other musicians had already done."

"That's so cool," Jilly said.

Clay noticed that Maddie was eyeing the grand piano. He bent down near her ear. "It's a beaut, isn't it? Have you ever played a grand piano before?"

Maddie shook her head. "Where would I play something that nice?"

He took Tony aside a moment, and they came back to Maddie. "Come on. The producer said you can see the piano."

Maddie looked like she was about to protest, but the temptation was too strong. She followed Clay into the studio, with

Jilly and Coop trailing behind. Slowly, Maddie walked up to the piano and tentatively touched the polished wood.

"Open the keyboard cover," Clay urged.

Maddie hesitated, then opened it up. The keys looked as if they'd never been touched.

"It's so beautiful," Maddie said, staring at it in awe.

A voice came over the speaker from the control room. "Go ahead and play a song. I'll record it for you."

Maddie backed up a step. "I can't."

"Of course you can," Clay said. "Here." He pulled his guitar from its case and brought the chair closer to the piano. "Let's play 'Colour My World' together. It'll be fun."

Maddie stared longingly at the piano. "I don't know it very well."

"Yes, you do," Jilly piped up. "You know it. Go ahead."

"I'd like to hear you play," Coop added.

Maddie took a deep breath, and Clay was afraid she'd bolt for the door. But instead, she stepped closer to the piano, pulled out the bench seat, and sat down.

"Any time you're ready," the soundman said.

"Go ahead, Madds. You start, and I'll play along," Clay urged.

Maddie raised her hands over the keyboard, then set her fingers gently on them. She hesitated a second, then began playing the intro to the song. The piano's tone was sweet and smooth, and Maddie played the song expertly. Clay watched her fingers move over the keys in wonder. This was his daughter playing so beautifully. His heart filled with pride. He began to strum his guitar, and they sounded perfect together, as if they'd practiced it.

When they came to the melody line, Clay began to sing. A

microphone hung above them, capturing the timeless words to the song:

"As time goes on, I realize, just what you mean, to me."

It was so hauntingly beautiful that everyone watched them in silent awe. When the last note was played, Maddie looked up at Clay, a tear in her eye. He smiled, and she smiled back. For that one instant, Clay felt a connection with Maddie. Then Coop and Jilly began clapping, and it broke the spell between father and daughter.

"That was amazing," Coop said, giving Maddie a squeeze. He looked at Clay. "You have a true musician in the family."

"Yes, we do," he said proudly.

A voice boomed over the speaker. "Beautiful! Come in here before you leave, and I'll give you a CD of it."

"Really?" Maddie said, looking at Clay. "A real recording of us."

"Of course," he said. "And recorded by the best in the business."

They stopped in the booth after Clay packed up his guitar, and as promised, the soundman gave them a CD and a memory stick with the song on it.

"So you can share it with your friends on Facebook," he told Maddie.

Maddie thanked him, as did Clay. Then they headed out into the late afternoon.

"Want to join us for dinner tonight?" Clay asked Coop.

"Thanks, man, but I'd better head out. I had a great time, though." He picked up Jilly and swung her around as she squealed with delight, and then he gave Maddie a hug.

"Don't be strangers, you two. I want to see you again real soon."

"Thanks for being here today," Clay told Coop. "You're a good friend."

"I know, aren't I?" Coop teased. He waved and left.

Clay was thrilled the day had gone so well. He felt that today had brought him and Maddie closer.

Chapter Fifteen

The trio dropped off Clay's guitar at home and then headed out to dinner. They drove to a place across the street from the beach and ate outside at a table with a blue-and-white-striped umbrella.

"I can't wait to hear the recording from today," Clay said as they waited for their food.

"Can we play it for Mom when we get back?" Jilly asked. "She would love hearing it."

"I think that's a wonderful idea," he said. "What do you think, Madds?"

Maddie nodded but stayed quiet. The food came, and Clay and Jilly were the ones who did all the talking. Afterward, they went back to the apartment, since they wanted to leave early in the morning for home. Once there, Clay called Eileen to ask how Jess was doing.

"She's still the same," Eileen reported. "I wish I had good news for you, but nothing has changed."

"Thanks, Eileen. We'll see you tomorrow." He hung up. "Mom's still the same," he told the girls. "But she's sure to perk up when she hears Maddie playing her favorite song."

Jilly nodded enthusiastically, but Maddie just sat on the sofa, still silent. Clay walked over and sat down next to her.

"What's the matter, Madds? You've been so quiet. I thought you had fun today."

Maddie turned sad eyes to him. "I did. I mean, it was fun going to the studio and seeing Uncle Coop and playing the piano."

"But?"

"There was really no reason for us to come here. Jilly and I could have stayed with the Neilsons and not have missed school. I'm just wondering why you brought us along."

"I thought you might like coming along. It's been a while since you've gone to the studio with me. I thought it might bring back some good memories from when you lived here before," Clay said.

She shook her head. "That's not why you brought us here. I think the real reason is you wanted us to like it here. Because if Mom doesn't wake up, you'll want to bring us here to live so you can work."

He stared at her, dumbfounded. "That's not it at all. And don't say that your mom isn't going to wake up. She will. I know it."

"You don't really believe that. You keep saying it, but I know you don't believe it. You're already thinking of what you're going to do when she dies."

"Stop it, Maddie. Don't say that! Your mother will wake up."

Maddie crossed her arms and stared straight ahead.

He softened his tone. "Madds, listen. I thought bringing you here would remind you of the good times we had as a family and how close you and I once were. I had hoped it would bring us closer. I also didn't want to leave you two behind. I couldn't bear the thought of you both worrying that I wasn't coming back."

"I don't have to come here to remember the past," Maddie said. "I remember everything perfectly."

"What do you remember?" Clay asked.

"I remember it all," Maddie said softly. "The good times, and the bad. I used to go with you to the studio and see Uncle Coop. The other band guys came over to the house and played music for hours. I loved that. I remember walking the beach with you and Mom, and then with Jilly too, after she was born. I was happy. You were my hero, and I thought you could do anything."

Clay watched as Maddie's face grew tighter. "I also remember you leaving a lot, to play on the road, and to go to rehab. Of course, no one called it that. Mom said you were going somewhere to rest and feel better. I didn't really understand why you couldn't stay home and rest. I missed you. But at least you did come home—until the day you didn't."

Clay winced. It hurt to hear her say it that way. "Maddie. I've been trying so hard to prove to you that I'm back now and that I'm not going away. You're right—I had a motive for bringing you here other than to remind you of happier times. I wanted to prove to you that I was going to return. If I'd left you with Eileen, I was afraid you'd worry that I wasn't coming back. Bringing you and Jilly along was the perfect way for us to spend time together. As a family. That's what we are—a family. I made a huge mistake last time, but I swear I'll do everything in my power to be the best dad I can be now. Just like before."

Maddie shook her head.

Clay drew closer to her on the sofa. "Madds. Please. What can I do to prove to you that I'm telling the truth? Yes, there will be times when I'll have to go off to work, but I'll always come home to you and Jilly and your mom. How can I make you believe that?"

"You can't," Maddie said, getting up and walking away from him. "I'll never be able to trust you. Every time you leave, to work at a studio or play on the road, I'll always think you won't come back. Always."

She walked into the bedroom, shutting the door quietly.

Clay felt like he'd been punched in the stomach. He'd lost Maddie's trust forever.

"Daddy?" Jilly came up to him and touched his arm.

Turning, he gazed into his little girl's sweet blue eyes.

"I believe in you," she said quietly. "Maddie will too. Just keep trying to show her."

Her words softened the blow that Maddie had just dealt him. "Thank you, sweetie. I really needed to hear that."

She smiled and then headed into the bedroom.

Later, as Clay lay on the sofa and sleep eluded him, he thought about all that Maddie had said. He'd failed her three times, the last time by not returning like he'd promised. Through it all, Jess had continued to believe in him, but Maddie no longer did. And that tore at his very soul.

How could he blame her? Wouldn't he have felt just as betrayed if he'd been in her shoes? There was no excuse. He'd made a huge mistake, and no one but him could clean up his mess.

* * *

2009–2011

After Jilly was born, life became even more chaotic for Clay and Jess. Maddie had started kindergarten a few days before the baby's arrival. A week after Jilly was born, Clay went on the road for six weeks with a country western band. He'd wanted to cancel and stay home with Jess and the girls, but he'd signed a contract almost a year before and couldn't get out of it. Always supportive, Jess took it all in stride.

"We'll send you pictures and be here waiting for you when you come home," she'd told him.

She'd looked tired but had smiled at him just the same. So off he went, and even though he'd been good at home about not drinking, it all went downhill the longer he was on the road. Endless hours on a tour bus with nothing to do and long nights of playing, packing up, and riding again made drinking an easy escape.

When he returned home, he found it hard to give up drinking all hours of the day and night. Jilly was a beautiful baby, but she didn't sleep well. She was up every two to four hours, making it impossible for Jess or Clay to get any sleep. Clay helped as much as he could, getting up at night to feed Jilly and rock her back to sleep, but would then reward himself by having a few beers. Then he'd be up early to drive Maddie to school while Jess cared for the baby.

He loved his children dearly, but life was more stressful now that there was another child in the house. And being the sole breadwinner, he worried constantly about earning enough money to support his family, so he took every studio and road job that came his way.

Several times Jess caught him drinking while he cared for the baby, and she admonished him for it.

"You know how I feel about drinking while watching the girls," she told him angrily.

"But it's just *one* beer," he'd tell her, brushing it aside as her being overprotective. Of course, that was a lie. He'd have three or four and hide the empties out in the trash in the garage.

It wasn't unusual for Clay to drink too much while working at the studio. Knowing that Jess wouldn't approve of his driving home after drinking, he'd sneak into the house and crawl into bed to sleep it off. But one night, when he came stumbling in at four in the morning, Jess was awake, rocking the baby to sleep. The look on her face said it all—she knew he'd been driving drunk, and she was furious. But she sat there, silent, as he crept into their bedroom and passed out. The next morning, though, she let him know how she felt.

It was a Saturday, so Maddie was watching cartoons and eating her cereal, and Jilly was in her playpen having a late morning nap when Clay stumbled into the kitchen for coffee. He was sure he looked as bad as he felt. But when he saw Jess's face tighten, he knew he was in for it.

She stood and left the room, and he followed her into the bedroom.

"I'm sorry about last night," he said. "It was a long day at the studio, and I had a couple of beers. You know how tedious those recording sessions can be."

Jess turned and glared at him. "You were driving drunk—again! There's no excuse for that. You could have called a cab to bring you home or slept it off at the studio."

"Hon, it wasn't that bad. I only had a couple of beers. I was just tired from eighteen hours in the studio," he said, lying.

Her blue eyes flashed. "You reeked like a brewery, and you were stumbling around. Don't lie to me, Clay. It just makes it worse. The drinking is bad enough, but drunk driving? What if you'd been in an accident? What would the girls and I do then? Why can't you think of someone else besides yourself for a change?"

He was stunned. He couldn't believe she was calling him selfish. "How can you say that? All I do is think about you and the girls. Why do you think I work so much? It's for all of you. If I have a few beers now and again, so what? I have to let off steam somehow."

His voice had raised, and he saw Jess's face grow angrier by the second.

"Don't you dare blame your drinking on us. You choose to work that much. We would be fine if you worked less, and you know that. You're choosing work and alcohol over your family. We both know that, so why don't you just come out and admit it!"

Clay stared at her, unable to think straight. They'd never had such an ugly fight before, and he couldn't believe what Jess was accusing him of. He put his family first. How could she say that he was choosing alcohol over them?

Before he could reply, he heard a small noise in the doorway. He and Jess both turned, and there stood Maddie, still wearing her Hello Kitty pajamas and fuzzy pink slippers.

"Can we go to the park today, Daddy?" she asked, her eyes wide.

Clay wondered how much she'd heard and suddenly felt ashamed for fighting with Jess.

"Sure we can, sweetie," he said, his voice now calm. "Let Daddy get showered and dressed; then we can go. And let's take Jilly too and give your mommy a break."

Maddie smiled and shuffled back to the living room.

Feeling horrible, he turned back to Jess.

"I'm so sorry," he said softly. "I don't know what got into me. I don't want to fight. You're right. I wasn't thinking of anyone but myself. I promise I'll do better."

She looked at him, her expression pained. "You keep telling me that, but it hasn't gotten better. Please, Clay. I can't do this much longer. You have to stop drinking, or something terrible is going to happen."

"I promise I will. I'll stop. Please believe me, sweetie. I can do this," he said, meaning every word.

After another year of broken promises to quit drinking, Jess gave Clay an ultimatum—stop drinking, or she and the children would leave. So in May 2011, Clay went to rehab for the very first time.

* * *

Present

Clay and the girls headed home the next morning. Like the drive down, the drive back was quiet. His hopes of bonding with Maddie had been dashed. If anything, he felt even further away from her. He'd run out of ways to prove to her that he loved her. She just wasn't ready to listen, and that hurt him deeply.

They arrived home around four in the afternoon, and Maddie immediately went upstairs to her room. Jilly also went upstairs to put her things away, but it wasn't long before she found her father in the kitchen.

"Can we go visit Mom tonight?" she asked. "We can bring the CD and play it for her."

Clay looked into his daughter's hopeful eyes. He knew she thought that somehow the music would magically wake her mom up, and as much as he wished it too, he had to be more realistic than that.

"Are you sure you want to get back into the car after the long drive home?" he asked, hoping she'd say no. He didn't have the energy for any more disappointments.

"Please, Daddy? I want to see Mom."

He couldn't resist her. "Okay, sweetie. Why don't you ask your sister if she wants to go? We can eat dinner at the hospital."

Jilly smiled and ran off to ask Maddie. Soon, both girls came downstairs. Jilly carried a small CD player.

They were at the hospital forty-five minutes later. Just as Eileen had reported, nothing had changed. Jess was still lying peacefully on the bed, still using the ventilator to breathe.

Clay kissed Jess's forehead.

"Hey, sweetie. We're back," he said softly.

Maddie sat in her usual chair but made no attempt to talk to her mom. Jilly, however, was excited and immediately told her mother all about their trip, about watching her dad record in the studio and how Maddie and Dad had played a song together.

"You have to hear this song, Mom," Jilly said enthusiastically. "Maddie played piano, and Dad played guitar and sang. It's your favorite song. You're going to love it."

She gently set the CD player on the bed and put in the disc. Then she hit play.

After a moment of silence, the piano intro started, and then the guitar began strumming along. Maddie played beautifully, and Clay's guitar added depth to the melody. But when Clay began to sing, it became a hauntingly beautiful song that tore at the heartstrings.

As he listened to the mixture of his daughter's soulful playing and the poignant lyrics, tears filled Clay's eyes. He glanced at Jilly, watching her mother expectantly. *She really believes that this song will wake Jess up.*

His heart broke for his daughter. He wished it was as simple as playing a song to bring Jess back to them. Glancing at Maddie, he saw her wiping away tears. It was an incredibly heartwrenching moment for all three of them; they so desperately wanted Jess to come back.

A small gasp came from within the room, and all eyes turned to Jess. But she was lying there, silent.

"I'm sorry," a voice said from behind them.

All three turned and saw a nurse standing near the door.

"I came in to check your wife's vitals, and when I heard the music, I stopped. It was so beautiful," the nurse said.

The song had ended, and Jilly clicked off the player, disappointment marring her young face.

Clay stood. "We'll get out of your way for a while. Let's go have dinner, girls."

Silently, they filed out of the room. Inside the elevator, Jilly erupted in a flood of tears.

"Oh, Jilly-bear." Clay kneeled down to hug her as she cried.

"I . . . thought . . . Mommy . . . would . . . wake . . . up," his daughter stuttered through her tears.

"I know, baby. I know. I'm so sorry. I really wanted the song to wake her up too," Clay said, his own emotions tearing him apart inside.

He wanted to put his fist through a wall, or run down the halls screaming his anger. Instead, he lifted Jilly up into his arms, and when the elevator doors opened on the cafeteria's floor, he carried her to a bench by the wall and sat down, still cradling her.

Maddie followed and placed a comforting hand on Jilly's back.

"I wanted Mom to wake up too," she said softly. "But you tried. And we can keep trying, okay?"

Clay looked over Jilly's head and into Maddie's teary eyes. She wasn't angry or resentful. She was Jilly's big sister, who wanted to help make her feel better. Clay couldn't have been prouder of Maddie at that moment.

Jilly finally calmed down, and they went into the cafeteria. None of them were hungry at that point, but he urged the girls to eat something, even telling them they could eat dessert first as a special treat. Both girls looked shocked, especially Maddie, but it cheered them up, and they took him up on it. Jilly ate chocolate pudding before her chicken nuggets, and Maddie ate a big chocolate chip cookie. The girls even giggled as their father ate a piece of apple pie before eating his sandwich. After eating, they went back to say good night to Jess, then left the hospital and drove home. They were all physically and emotionally exhausted. Jilly fell asleep on the ride home, and Maddie sat quietly gazing out the window. Clay was also lost in his thoughts as he drove along the highway.

He'd wanted to believe in the magic of the moment as much as Jilly had. Jess's favorite song played so beautifully by her beloved daughter. How could that not have brought Jess back? Musicians wanted to believe that their music was magical. That a song could heal all wounds and heartbreak. Of course, in reality, it couldn't. But how lovely a dream it was. And how devastating dreaming could be.

Once home, Clay carefully lifted Jilly in his arms and carried her up the long staircase to her room. Maddie slipped off Jilly's shoes and pulled her blankets back. Then her father gently laid her on her bed and covered her up.

"What about her pajamas?" Maddie whispered.

"We'll let her sleep in her clothes. I'd hate to wake her. She's had a rough night."

She nodded as Clay headed for the door.

He turned and looked at Maddie. "Thanks for being so kind to Jilly."

Maddie shrugged. "She's my baby sister. It's my job to be nice to her."

He smiled. "And you're my daughter. I love you, Madds. I always have and always will. I hope you will believe that someday."

"It's not your love that I doubt," she said, looking up at him with tired eyes. "It's whether or not you'll stay."

"Fair enough. Good night, Madds," he said, then softly closed the door.

Chapter Sixteen

2011–2012

After one month of rehab, Clay came home feeling healthier and thinking clearer than he had in years. He was ready to return to his life with renewed energy. Unfortunately, life had thrown their family an unexpected curveball, and Clay came home to more stress than he could manage.

While he was in rehab, Jess's mother, Karen, had been diagnosed with stage 4 breast cancer and was immediately put on an aggressive treatment plan. Jess was taking her mother to doctor appointments while juggling the girls' summer schedules. Maddie was almost seven and had just started taking piano lessons and swimming classes. Jilly was a year and a half and was busy walking everywhere and getting into everything, needing constant supervision.

When Clay came home, he had no chance to slowly acclimate himself back into the daily family routine. In order to give Jess the time she needed to care for her mother, he had to immediately take over caring for the girls, which was stressful at times.

He loved his family; he just wasn't ready to jump into the middle of everything so quickly.

Maddie was also unusually clingy with her father, constantly following him everywhere and not wanting him to leave the house without her. She'd pout or cry if he left, even if it was for work, and wanted only him to do everything for her. She insisted that he drive her to piano lessons or swimming, and she would let only him take her to the park or beach. It was difficult for him to deal with her constant need for attention. Jess, herself under a lot of strain, told him to be patient.

"Maddie's just reacting to you having been gone. She'll calm down after you've been home a while," she said.

So he took Maddie along to many of his recording sessions, and to her credit, she did sit quietly in the corner of the control room and watch him intently as he played guitar. Clay, however, was dealing with stress from all sides. After losing an entire month of work from being at rehab, along with the high cost of the rehab stay itself, he knew he had to take all the jobs offered him.

But Maddie's clinginess and his being needed at home didn't make it easy for him to work. The entire environment wasn't conducive to staying sober, and after a few short weeks, he started drinking to relieve the pressure he felt. This time, though, he did a better job of hiding it from his wife. Overwhelmed with family needs and her mother's illness, Jess didn't seem to notice if Clay was a bit too happy, or walked a little wobbly at times. Clay wasn't sure if she knew or not, or if she just ignored it, too exhausted to deal with him along with everything else.

Despite his drinking, Clay still worked, cared for the girls, and helped around the house as much as possible to make Jess's life a little easier.

It's not a problem. I've got this. At least that's what he told himself.

Almost a year after Karen had been diagnosed in April 2012, she lost her battle with cancer. It had been a long, emotional year for all of them, and Clay felt not only sadness over Karen's death but also deep compassion for his wife. It was Jess who planned the funeral, packed up her mother's house, and took care of the sale of it. With only her grandmother to consult with over decisions, it was a huge responsibility for Jess to dismantle her mother's life and say good-bye to her all at once. Jess's anxiety spilled over to Clay as well. It soon became more than he could handle. But as usual, he and Jess forged on, together.

* * *

Present

The next day, much to his surprise, the girls were up at their regular time and got ready for school. He mentioned to them at breakfast that they could stay home if they felt tired after their long day, but they decided to go. There was only a month and a half left of school, and they didn't want to miss any more.

Clay was proud that both of his daughters were so dedicated to their schoolwork. He could certainly learn a lot from them.

He drove to the hospital and sat all morning with Jess. Most of the time was spent talking to her, telling her how talented Maddie was on the piano, gushing over Jilly's sweet personality and swimming ability, and reporting how much work they'd finished on the house so far. He hoped that something in what he was saying would spark a response in his wife, but nothing happened. Still, he talked on, because he had to believe she heard him and eventually something he said would trigger a response.

In the early afternoon, Dr. Bradbury came in to check on Jess. Clay was glad to see him, hoping that he'd have news on her condition.

The doctor shook his head. "I'm sorry, but nothing has changed. I've tried taking her off of the ventilator several times, but to no avail. We've done every scan imaginable, yet nothing shows up. Her brain is functioning normally, so there doesn't seem to be any damage. It's just a waiting game at this stage."

Clay sighed. "We've been waiting for three weeks, and nothing positive has happened. Can't you give me any idea at all if there's a possibility she will or will not wake up?" He was desperate for any news—good or bad—at this point. It would be better to know than to simply keep waiting.

"I'm sorry. Every patient is different. One can be in a coma a few days and wake up; another won't wake for weeks. There's still a good chance your wife will wake up any day now. Or even in a few more weeks. All we can do is wait."

Clay wondered how other people continued to move on with their lives while waiting for a loved one to wake from a coma. Do you keep living as you normally would and hope they'll wake up? Or do you put everything on hold until they do?

As he drove home, he thought of Maddie and how she wanted to finish the work on the house for her mother. At first, he'd thought it would be a waste of time. But now, he wondered if it was the right thing to do. If—no, *when*—Jess woke up, the place would be ready for her. But what if she didn't wake up for weeks, or months, or years?

"Stop thinking that," he said. "She will wake up. She has to!"

Right then and there, he made his decision. He'd proceed with the B&B for Jess, and even if she didn't wake up in time for Memorial Day weekend, he would open it just the same. He was a musician, not an innkeeper, but he could continue to play music for a living no matter what happened. He was determined to do this for Jess. He believed that moving forward with opening the B&B would keep their faith alive that Jess was coming back to them.

He picked up subs for dinner and headed home. The girls were walking over from Eileen's house when he stepped out of his car.

"Hey there. I brought dinner home," he said cheerfully, lifting the bag so they could see.

As they ate, Clay told the girls his plans. "I've decided to open the house to guests even if you mother hasn't woken up by Memorial Day. We'll keep fixing the place up and have it ready."

Maddie's eyebrows rose. "I thought you didn't want to open it without Mom."

"I was hesitant, that's true. But now I want to. Your Mom will be so happy that we continued with her plans when she does wake up," he said.

Maddie grinned. "Okay. We'll keep working. We still have to order the furniture she wanted for the last two bedrooms, and there's still a few finishing touches left. We also have to plant the flowers around the house the way she wanted. And what about making breakfast for the guests? Who will cook?"

He frowned. He'd forgotten about the *breakfast* part of *B&B*. "I'm not sure what we'll do about that. I'll have to think about it. But we're still moving forward."

His older daughter nodded, obviously pleased. But Jilly didn't look convinced.

"Dad? What if Mommy doesn't wake up for a long time? Will you still want to stay here and do this? Don't you want to play music?"

Both Clay and Maddie looked at her with surprise. He had thought that Maddie would be the one to bring up the fact that he wouldn't want to run a B&B for the rest of his life.

"Well, sweetie, I'm not sure I can answer that right now. I still believe that your mommy is coming back to us. I don't want to think any other way. If something changes, then we'll decide what to do as a family, okay?"

Jilly nodded and stared down at her plate.

Her father placed a finger under her chin and raised her eyes to his. "Are you going to help me plant the flowers around the house?"

Jilly's eyes lit up. She nodded vigorously.

"Good. I'll need your help," he said, smiling again. He looked at both girls. "So, are we in this together? As a family?"

Both girls yelled an enthusiastic *yes*, and he gave them each a high five.

Maddie rolled her eyes. "That's so lame."

But Clay saw her smiling.

* * *

Eileen and her children came over just as Clay was leaving to go to his AA meeting.

"The girls seem happier," Eileen commented quietly to Clay at the door. "What happened?"

"We made a plan to continue everything the way Jess wanted it. We'll open as a B&B on Memorial Day weekend no matter what happens."

"I see. Well, I think that's a good plan. Jess has put a lot of work into this place. I think she'd be pleased knowing that you're continuing her work."

"I agree. It will keep the girls busy too and keep them thinking positive. I'm afraid if we don't keep moving forward, we'll lose hope."

Eileen nodded. "Have you thought about who will cook for you if you do open without Jess?"

"That's the big hiccup in the plan," he said. "I have to figure out something."

"The local bakery makes a delicious variety of breakfast pastries. They'll cater too. You could have them add cut-up fruit and juice and such. Or you and the girls could do that part. It's something to think about," Eileen said.

"That's a good idea. Thanks. It would eliminate the need to hire a cook," Clay said, feeling relieved.

"But, of course, we are hoping Jess will be here instead," Eileen said.

He smiled. "Yes, we are. But it's good to have an alternate plan."

When Clay arrived at the AA meeting, Alex was already there, setting up the coffee and cookies. Clay offered to help and went to work.

"How are you doing?" Alex asked as he put out cups and plates.

"As well as can be expected," Clay said. "I just told Eileen that the girls and I are going to move forward with the B&B plan for Jess's sake. She helped me solve one of our obstacles too. Your wife is an amazing person."

"I have to agree with you there," Alex said, chuckling.

The meeting started, and for the first time since arriving in town, Clay felt optimistic. He stood and spoke about what had been going on in his life over the past week and how he and his daughters were staying positive and moving forward. He wanted to share this with the group so they could see that even when things were tough, you can still make the best of the situation.

When he arrived home, the sound of a piano and violin floated out into the cool night. Stepping inside the house as quietly as he could, he paused in the entryway, listening. Maddie played "Colour My World" perfectly, and even though Emma struggled to keep up, she was doing quite well for having just learned it.

When the music stopped, there was clapping in the living room. He smiled. Despite trying so hard not to be, his daughter was very much like him.

"I know you're out there, so you may as well come in here," Maddie's voice called out.

He sheepishly came around the corner. "Sorry. I didn't want you to stop. You both play so beautifully, I had to listen."

Maddie stared at him a moment, her eyes serious. Clay thought for sure she was mad at him, but then she said, "Well?"

His brow wrinkled. "Well what?"

"You know you want to play along with us, so come on."

"Really?"

Maddie gave a big dramatic sigh. "I wouldn't have asked if I didn't mean it."

Clay glanced over at Eileen, who gave him an encouraging smile, and then at Jilly, whose eyes lit up with excitement.

"Play, Dad. Please? And sing?"

Clay hesitated. He actually felt nervous.

"I'd like to hear you three play together too," Eileen added.

"I'm in," he said happily. After retrieving his guitar from his room, he pulled the desk chair over next to Emma. "Whenever you're ready, Maestro," he said to Maddie.

His daughter started playing the beautiful intro, and soon

Emma's violin joined in, and then Clay played, adding a rich fullness to the song. When he sang the soulful lyrics, the room became still, as all eyes and ears were on him. He didn't notice as he sang, but when the song ended, he realized that everyone was staring at him in awe. Jilly's eyes sparkled, Jerrod stared at him with wonder, and Eileen was brushing a tear from her cheek.

"Lovely," Eileen finally said. "Absolutely beautiful."

Eileen pulled herself together and announced it was time to leave. Emma packed up her violin, and Jerrod helped Jilly pick up the game they'd played earlier. Once they were at the door, Clay thanked Eileen for once again helping with the kids.

"My pleasure," she said. She hesitated at the door, then said, "I knew you were a musician, but I didn't know how talented you really were. What a wonderful surprise."

"Thank you," Clay said. A compliment from Eileen meant a lot to him. He knew she didn't hand them out often.

After the Neilsons left, Clay walked back into the living room. Jilly had run upstairs to get ready for bed. Maddie had already closed up the piano and was turning off the lamps.

"Hey, Madds?" he said. "Thanks for letting me play with you and Emma."

Maddie shrugged. "It was no big deal."

"Yes, it was," Clay said. "It was a huge deal to me."

Maddie walked toward the stairs, then turned toward him. "So, this weekend we get to work on the house again?"

"Yes. We'll make everything exactly as your Mom wanted it."

"Okay." She headed up the first few steps.

Clay drew closer. "Good night, Madds."

Maddie stopped a moment, seeming to consider.

"Good night, Dad," she finally said before running up the stairs. His heart felt full.

Chapter Seventeen

For the next two nights, he and the girls went to visit Jess after school. Jilly tried talking to her mom but soon grew discouraged. Maddie did too. Nothing they said elicited the reaction they wanted. Despite their excitement over the prospect of finishing the house, they still wanted only one thing—for their mom to wake up. But there was no sign of it happening. So they soon fell into silence, reading or working on their homework.

Clay hated to see them lose faith, but he understood their feelings. He realized it had only been three weeks, but that was a long time for those left waiting. He hoped that once they started working on the house again, it would renew their faith in Jess's coming back to them.

The next morning, Maddie was already up and working on the yellow room when Clay came upstairs. She'd enlisted Jilly's services to help with the taping and laying down plastic on the carpeting. He was delighted that Maddie had included her sister.

"It looks like you have this room under control," Clay said cheerfully. "I was wondering about the furniture, Madds. You said your mother ordered it online?"

She nodded. "I have a list of the things she wanted for the blue room and the yellow room."

"Maybe we should order it today. I assume it takes a while to get here," he said.

"Not long," Maddie said. "A week or so. But you have to put most of it together, and that takes a long time."

"What? I have to put together furniture? Who did it for your mom?"

"She did most of it. Mr. Neilson came over and helped her with the heavy stuff. She put together all the bedroom furniture."

Clay figured he'd need help from Alex too. "Well, why don't we go order it now, and then you can work on this room later?"

Maddie set her things down. "Come on, Jilly. You can help me order the furniture."

Jilly smiled brightly and came running.

"Thanks for letting Jilly help," he said as he followed her downstairs. "You're a good sister."

She shrugged. "I don't mind her helping."

He smiled. Maddie could be moody and contrary and sullen toward him, but she was a good sister to Jilly. He knew, deep down, that she had a kind heart, and her anger with him was a front to keep him at arm's length.

Someday, I'll break through that wall she's put up against me. Hopefully sooner rather than later.

There was a long list of furniture for the two rooms, and it was after noon by the time they'd placed the entire order. Clay suggested they go see Jess and have dinner afterward. Then they could work on the house awhile that evening. Maddie agreed, but Jilly was hesitant.

"Do we have to go to the hospital today?" Jilly asked, looking down.

"Of course we have to go," her sister said, irritated. "Mom will want to see us."

Jilly looked up at Maddie with sad eyes. "Mom doesn't know we're there."

Maddie frowned and was about to reply when Clay placed a gentle hand on her shoulder to stop her.

Kneeling down, he looked Jilly in the eye. "Don't you want to see your mom?"

A tear rolled down her cheek. "Mom can't hear us. She just sleeps and doesn't know we're there. Why can't we stay here and work on the house?"

"Sweetie, I know it's disheartening seeing your mom lie there and not respond, but the doctor and nurses all believe she can hear us when we talk to her," he said tenderly. "Let's go for a little while so she knows we're there, and then we can come home, okay?"

More tears fell. "I hate seeing Mom that way. It scares me."

"Ah, sweetie." Clay wrapped his arms around her. "I know this is hard. It's hard for all of us. But we can't give up on your mom. Okay?"

Maddie moved closer to them. "You have to come, Jilly. Maybe we can stop at your favorite place for chicken nuggets afterward, and then I'll let you help me some more on the yellow room."

Jilly looked from Maddie to her dad, wiping the tears from her face. "Can I get chicken nuggets for dinner, Dad?"

He smiled. "Of course you can."

"Okay," she agreed. "Maybe I can tell Mom that I'm helping with the yellow room."

"Sure you can," Maddie said, taking Jilly's hand. "And that we ordered furniture, and you hit the 'Order' button."

Jilly smiled up at her sister. "Okay."

Clay watched as Maddie led her sister out into the entryway. His heart was a tangle of emotions. He was proud of the sweet way Maddie treated Jilly, but he was sad that Jilly hadn't wanted to see her mother.

How much longer before both girls give up on Jess? How much longer before he *did?* He couldn't bear to think of it.

With a sigh, he followed the girls out the door.

* * *

2012–2013

The summer after Karen's death, Jess decided to take the girls up to her grandmother's house in Northern California for a couple of weeks to decompress. Clay had agreed it was a good idea—the girls hadn't seen much of their great-grandmother except at the funeral, and he had a two-week stint on the road during that time anyway. They could all take a breather and hopefully come back feeling refreshed. But being on the road with a rock band did not help him drink any less. He was proud of himself for not touching drugs of any kind or drinking hard liquor, but he drank beer freely and, more nights than not, ended up passed out in his bunk on the bus. Each day he'd tell himself he could stop, and each day he failed. He promised himself that as soon as he was home again, he'd quit cold turkey. He didn't want Jess to be disappointed in him—again.

But once they were all back home, the drinking continued. Jess knew he was drinking, but he told her he had it under control, didn't drive drunk, and only had a couple of beers here and there.

"I'm too busy to monitor your drinking," Jess told him one evening after the kids were in bed, when they were lying together on the sofa, enjoying the silence. She looked tired, like she just couldn't take on one more problem. "I have to trust you when you say you have control over it."

Clay reassured her that he did, but as time went on, his thirst grew stronger. On days he was home, he tried to hold back and not drink a drop, but by noon he had the shakes, and by five he was a basket case. He started drinking at home in the evenings. Then it became more prominent in the afternoons. More and more, Jess wouldn't let him take the girls to the beach or the park.

"I'll drive them," she told him, disappointment showing in her eyes.

Although Clay fought the urge to drink, he always lost. *I'm not like my dad!* he'd insist to himself, but the truth was, he was turning into his father.

Drinking became more important than being with his family. He spent longer hours than necessary at the studio, even going there when he had no job lined up. He'd meet his friends in a bar and not come home until late at night, long after Jess had gone to bed. He was missing out on his life with his children and his wife—yet he didn't know how to find his way back.

"I miss you," Jess said softly one night as he crawled into bed after being at the studio late.

He reached out and curled his body around hers.

"I'm sorry I'm gone so much," he whispered in her ear. "It'll get better, I promise."

"Do you really need to work so much? We're not wanting for money, Clay. We have enough money. It's you we need. The girls miss you being home as much as I do."

"I'm sorry," he said again.

Jess rolled over on her back and stared up at the ceiling. "I miss the days when being together was all that mattered. When we spent the day together doing nothing important, just being together."

He kissed her ear. "I miss those days too."

She turned her head to face him. "It's not work that's taking you away from us. It's your drinking. I know you think you're hiding it, but it's getting worse. Maybe it's time you get help again."

Clay sighed. "It's not that bad. I can stop any time I want to."

"Oh, honey," Jess said with a sigh.

Guilt washed over Clay. He was hurting his wife, his girls, and himself. He knew that, but it still wasn't enough to make him stop. He leaned over Jess and kissed her softly on the lips.

"I'll try harder, I promise. I love you and the girls more than anything."

Jess turned sad eyes on him. "I don't doubt your love, not for one minute. But I'm not sure how much more I can take of your drinking. I just want you back, Clay. Like you were before drinking took you from me. Can't you stop, for no other reason than because I need you?"

"I'll try. I promise. I'll try harder," he said, wrapping his arms around her again. "Don't give up on me, Jess. I don't know what I'd do without you."

"I won't give up on you," she said softly.

Clay wanted more than anything to make Jess happy. He'd meant what he said, but keeping his promise was much harder than he ever imagined.

In late December, before Maddie's school let out for Christmas break, the children were putting on a holiday show for the parents. Maddie was set to play a solo of "Jingle Bells" on the piano and was so excited to have her parents see her on stage.

"I'm going to be just like you, Daddy!" she exclaimed gleefully. "I'm playing a song on stage, like you do."

Clay was proud of her. He'd heard her practice on their small electric piano and marveled at how well she played. The day of the program, he had to work at the studio for a few hours but promised Maddie he'd be there in time to hear her solo that evening. They made plans for him to meet them at the auditorium before the show began.

Right before the lights dimmed, Clay stumbled down the aisle, looking for Jess. He tripped once, righted himself, and finally saw her sitting up near the front. When he sat down beside her, she glared at him.

"Where have you been? You didn't answer my texts."

"I'm here now," he slurred.

"You're drunk. How could you come here like that?"

"I only had a couple," he said, then crossed his arms and scrunched down in his chair.

He didn't understand why she was so angry. He made it, and that was all that mattered.

Maddie's part came, and she played her song beautifully. Everyone clapped enthusiastically and cheered, but Clay stood and was the loudest, whistling and yelling. People turned and stared, and Jess had to pull him back down.

"Stop it! You'll embarrass her," she admonished him.

When the program was over, he made a big deal over Maddie in the school's common room, where cookies and punch were being served.

"A chip off the old block," he said loudly. "She's a musician, just like her dad."

He stumbled around and spilled punch all over the floor, causing Maddie to turn red with embarrassment. Jess pulled him outside and insisted he ride home with them.

"I can drive," he said indignantly.

"You're drunk," Jess said angrily, but not so loudly that the girls could hear. "Don't you dare drive home."

Finally he relented. Once home, he quickly passed out on their bed.

The next morning, Clay felt awful when Jess told him how he'd behaved in front of Maddie, Jilly, and the entire school.

"I'm so sorry, Jess. I didn't realize I'd had one too many."

"You drove drunk again last night," Jess said. "You keep doing it no matter how many times I ask you not to. You're going to kill someone, or yourself."

"I can do better. Believe me. I'll stop, I promise. Please don't be angry with me," he begged.

He hated seeing the disappointment in her eyes. He didn't know why he couldn't stop himself from being so irresponsible. He knew better than to drive drunk, and yet he continued to do it.

Tears filled Jess's eyes. "How many more times will you say that, and it won't be true? You have to go back to rehab, Clay. Please. I can't do this anymore."

Clay hugged her tight. "I can do this without rehab. I can. I'll stop."

But despite his promises, Clay couldn't control his drinking, and once again in February 2013, he found himself in a rehab facility—except this time he was there for ten weeks.

Clay was determined for it to work this time. He did everything he was told, attended all the meetings and group sessions, and even began running again. He ran every day and increased his distance little by little until he was running five miles every morning. He felt healthier than he ever had in his life, and his thirst for alcohol decreased. He thought for sure that this time he could stop drinking for good.

When he finally came home, he continued his running routine each morning and was able to stay sober. He went to AA meetings every week and felt he'd finally kicked his addiction. Maddie, however, was upset with him. She hadn't been told exactly why he'd been gone, and it angered her that he'd leave them for so long. At first, she barely acknowledged his presence, and that broke Clay's heart. But slowly, as the weeks went by, he won her over again.

"Promise you won't leave us again," Maddie said one day as they walked the beach holding hands. Jess was a few steps behind, watching Jilly.

"I'll do my best, Madds, but I can't promise. Sometimes I'll be gone for work. But I'll try not to be gone so long ever again."

"Good," Maddie said, making Clay smile.

In June, Clay and Jess celebrated their tenth wedding anniversary. A friend watched the girls while they went out for dinner. Afterward, they found themselves on the beach where they'd first kissed, but this time there was no beer along.

They sat together on the sand as they watched the sunset. Clay wrapped his arm around his wife and kissed her gently on the cheek.

"Ten years. It went by so fast. It hasn't always been easy, I know. Do you regret any of it?" he asked.

Jess stared lovingly into his eyes. "No, not one moment. I love you, Clay. I'll take the good with the bad as long as I can be with you, forever."

Clay hugged her close. "I love you too, Jess. I'm sorry about the times I let you down. I'll try to do better. I don't want to disappoint you or the girls again."

He meant every word; he just didn't know how hard it would be to keep his promise.

* * *

Present

Sunday morning, Clay and the girls were up early and went to the nursery to buy flowers for the yard. Maddie had Jess's list and diagram of the flowers she wanted and where she wanted them planted. He marveled at how organized Jess was. She knew exactly what she wanted, thankfully, and it was a huge help to have her notes.

Once home, diagram in hand, Clay and Jilly began planting flowers in pots and flower beds around the house, exactly as Jess wanted. Maddie went upstairs to continue painting the yellow room. They had four weeks to get the place ready before Memorial Day weekend, and both Clay and Maddie were determined to finish it all.

That afternoon, they went to visit Jess again. Jilly brought along a vase of lavender that they'd bought especially for Jess. She set it on the window ledge near the now-empty vases from flowers that had died.

"Your mom will like those," Clay told her. "They're her favorite flower. Hopefully, she can smell the scent."

Jilly smiled. She sat next to her mom and told her about the flowers she and her dad were planting and how they were following Jess's instructions. "It's going to look so pretty when you wake up, Mom. Everything is going to be exactly as you wanted it to be."

At dinner in the cafeteria that night, all three talked excitedly about how the work on the house was progressing.

"Wait until you have to build the furniture," Maddie said, a hint of a tease in her voice. "Mom swore a lot when she did it."

He laughed. "Your mom swore? Then I suggest you girls stay far away from me when I do it. If it made her swear, I'll be terrible."

The girls giggled, and they talked about school coming to a close in only a month's time and about Maddie and Emma's upcoming duet. It was a typical conversation for any other family, but for Clay, it was special. This was the first time they'd all sat and talked normally—no jibes from Maddie or tears from Jilly. He only wished that Jess could be there to see how far they'd come in the past few weeks. She'd be so proud of him.

Chapter Eighteen

Monday was another typical day, with Clay spending the day with Jess at the hospital and then getting home in time to make dinner for the girls before taking Jilly to swimming practice. Maddie went along as usual to help Jilly dry her hair and change afterward. They were getting used to their routine, so much so that it was becoming normal. Clay hated that it didn't include Jess, but he was happy the girls were accepting his presence.

Tuesday when Clay arrived at the hospital, he met Dr. Bradbury in the hallway.

"Good morning, Mr. Connors," the doctor said, shaking his hand. "I'm glad you're here. I'm going to try to take your wife off the ventilator again. It's been a week since I've tried, so I'm hoping we have better luck this time."

Clay followed the doctor into the room and watched as he reset the machine settings.

"Usually, our patient is awake, and we can tell them to try to take a deep breath to clear their lungs," Dr. Bradbury said. "But in your wife's case, we have to hope that the body will react on its own and she'll take a breath. If she doesn't within a set time period, I'll hook her back up to the machine."

Clay nodded. He felt his whole body tense with nervousness.

"Don't be alarmed if she suddenly coughs or sounds like she's choking. That's the reaction we want," the doctor said.

He was poised to unhook the tube attached to Jess. "Ready?"

"Ready," Clay said. He desperately hoped it would work. Breathing on her own would, at least, be an improvement.

The doctor unhooked the tube and stood back, waiting. Nothing happened for what seemed like a lifetime to Clay but was actually only a few seconds. Just as the doctor bent over Jess to reattach the tube, she shuddered. Her body tried taking in a breath; then she coughed. The doctor lifted her to a sitting position, and she coughed again. After a second, she took a deep breath, then another.

The doctor laid Jess back down and listened to her lungs and heart with his stethoscope. He smiled wide at Clay. "She's doing it. Your wife is breathing on her own."

Relief flooded through him as tears filled his eyes. She was breathing on her own. After all this time, he felt like they'd made progress. The doctor called in the nurse, and she detached the tubing from Jess's face, replacing it with only a small oxygen tube under her nose.

"I'm giving her oxygen to make sure she is getting enough with each breath," the doctor told Clay. "The nurses will monitor her progress and make sure she is breathing regularly and receiving enough oxygen. But it looks like your wife is doing fine."

He gave Clay a reassuring smile.

Clay walked the doctor to the door. "I'm surprised with all the coughing that Jess didn't wake up."

"Sometimes it's enough to jolt a patient awake, but not this time, I'm afraid. But don't let that worry you. She's breathing on her own again, and that's a positive sign. Now, we wait again."

Clay thanked the doctor and walked back over to Jess's bed. The nurse had finished removing the tubes and had rolled the machine to the side. He assumed they'd want to keep it there awhile in case she relapsed. He prayed that she didn't.

It was nice seeing Jess's face again without the strap and tubing. The oxygen tube was almost invisible compared to what she'd had before. She seemed to be breathing easily, as if the ventilator had never happened. He was relieved she could breathe on her own, and hoped this was the first step to recovery.

* * *

That afternoon when he saw the girls, he was thrilled to be able to tell them the good news about their mother. Both Maddie and Jilly were excited and wanted to see her right away. Hopping into the car, they all headed to the hospital, their hopes high. Clay was happy they had something positive to dwell on for a change. The past few weeks had been so hard on them all, and this was a refreshing change.

They visited with Jess for a while, then grabbed a bite of dinner before returning home. Jilly hugged her father extra hard when she said good night.

"I'm so happy Mommy is doing better," she said, smiling brightly. "Will she wake up soon?"

He didn't want to dampen her high spirits. "I'm hoping she will. Keep thinking positive, and hopefully it will come true."

Maddie was a little less optimistic about her mother's condition, but Clay had to give her credit for not saying anything negative to her sister. He supposed at Maddie's age, she was more realistic than Jilly. But he knew that she also hoped for the best.

"Before we go to bed, let's celebrate," he said, heading for the kitchen.

He pulled down three champagne glasses from the cupboard and headed to the refrigerator.

Maddie frowned. "You're not going to open a bottle of champagne, are you?"

He laughed. "Absolutely not. None of us are supposed to be drinking that stuff."

He pulled out a can of 7Up and a bottle of maraschino cherries. Then he poured a little 7Up in each glass and put a cherry in each one too.

"It's fizzy just like champagne, and sweet," Clay said.

He lifted his glass, and the girls followed suit. "To better days and your Mom coming home to us."

They clinked glasses and drank, Jilly giggling over the bubbles tickling her nose.

They all laughed. It felt really good to laugh.

* * *

On Wednesday night at the AA meeting, Clay was thrilled to report that Jess was breathing on her own again.

"It's a step in the right direction," he said, and everyone was happy for him.

"Another positive is you've been able to pull through this difficult situation and stay sober," Alex said.

"I have to admit that it's been tough at times, but yes, I have. One day at a time, right?" Clay said.

Everyone agreed. One day at a time.

The next two days, Clay visited Jess during the day and then brought the girls at night. The girls, however, were becoming restless during their visits with their mom and both asked to leave earlier than usual. Clay couldn't blame them since nothing had changed. They had lost their enthusiasm to talk to her, and Clay found that disheartening. On one hand it was wonderful that they were slowly accepting him as their father again, but it was only because Jess wasn't there for them anymore. And that broke his heart.

The furniture they'd ordered arrived quickly, just as Maddie had said. So on Saturday, Clay moved the smaller boxes that he could carry by himself into the blue room. The furniture they'd ordered for this room was mostly antique white with wicker accents. The bed had a heavy wood headboard attached to the frame. There was also a clothing armoire, two nightstands, and a highboy dresser. The armoire pieces came in two big boxes and were too heavy for Clay to carry up himself, so he ran next door and asked Alex if he could give a hand.

"Anything is better than mowing," Alex said with a laugh.

Soon, Eileen came over to see what they were up to, and so did their kids. Eileen quickly put Emma and Jerrod to work, cleaning and polishing the furniture around the house and vacuuming while she gave the kitchen and bathrooms a once-over. Maddie and Jilly were still finishing up painting the yellow bedroom. The house was a bevy of activity by midday, and by late afternoon, they were all in the kitchen, looking for a bite to eat.

"I'll order pizza," Eileen suggested to unanimous agreement.

As soon as it was delivered, the hungry group gathered to eat it.

"I never expected all this when I asked for help moving boxes," Clay said, laughing. "But I sure appreciate the help. We've been gone so much that keeping the house clean hasn't been a priority."

"Happy to do it," Eileen said. "The place should be nice and clean when you open Memorial Day weekend. How many guests are coming?"

Clay looked over at Maddie. She knew better than he did.

"We have three of the six bedrooms filled that weekend with two people in each room. Mom said she wouldn't be surprised if more called, or some came unexpectedly," Maddie said.

"Well, we'll sure be busy, won't we girls?" Clay asked.

"And Mom will be busy too," Jilly said.

Everyone grew quiet. "What do you mean, sweetie?" Clay asked.

"Won't Mom be here by then too? We can't run this place without Mom." His younger daughter looked at him hopefully.

He struggled for the right answer.

"I'm sure your mom is going to do her best to try to be here," Eileen said, coming to Clay's rescue. "And we're all going to pray every day that she will."

Jilly nodded, seemingly satisfied with her answer.

The party atmosphere in the room had vanished. Everyone finished eating and went back to their work. Clay helped Eileen clear the table and thanked her for answering Jilly's question. "I was caught off guard. I'm glad you stepped in."

"No problem," Eileen said. "Kids do that all the time." She smiled. "But I meant it. I know Jess wants to be here as much as we want her to be. We'll keep praying that she'll come back to us."

"You're a good friend. Jess is very lucky to have you."

"And the girls are lucky to have you," she said. "I know I gave you a hard time to begin with, but you're doing a great job. I'm glad you're here."

They all worked into the early evening and accomplished so

much more than the girls and Clay could have done on their own. It wasn't until their neighbors had left that Clay realized they hadn't gone to see Jess. More importantly, the girls hadn't asked to go, either.

Clay wasn't sure how he felt about that. He was happy they'd had such a great day without worry, but it made him sad that they'd forgotten Jess. He knew it was just one day, but he worried it could happen more and more as time went on.

Wake up, Jess. Please, wake up.

* * *

2013

The summer of 2013 was a difficult time for Clay. He was working on his sobriety, which was a job in itself. He attended weekly AA meetings along with his best friend and new sponsor, Coop. Coop had been a "drinking for fun" guy like Clay, but it had gotten out of control, costing him jobs and affecting his musical career. He'd gone to rehab in 2011, two months before Clay had, except Coop had been able to stay sober ever since. After Clay's last stint in rehab, he'd asked Coop to be his sponsor. His friend was more than happy to oblige, and he made sure Clay went to meetings regularly.

But even with his meetings and daily running routine, Clay thought about drinking nearly every minute of every day. And it didn't help that he was constantly at the studio for work, where people were always passing around alcohol. He knew he had to get used to others drinking around him, but it was hard. The only bright side was his reputation as a lead guitar player was rising, and it seemed as if every country and rock star wanted him to play on their albums. He was making more money than he'd ever dreamed possible and earning the recognition he'd always desired. It seemed ironic that the one thing he'd wanted all his life—being a famous guitar player—had come true, but it was also the thing that placed his sobriety in jeopardy. He had to play; it was as important to him as breathing. He just had to learn to work around people who drank and not let it tempt him.

Jess noticed how wound up he was after working and often asked him if he was doing okay.

"I'm not drinking, if that's what you're afraid of," he snapped one night as he was climbing into bed after a long recording session.

"I was just asking if you were all right," she said, turning over in bed.

His heart sank. He hated that he was so strung out that he became short with Jess. He drew near and wrapped his arms around her. "I'm sorry. I didn't mean to snap at you. I'm just tired, and when I'm at work, all I can think about is having a beer and relaxing."

Clay had been honest with Jess about his cravings so she'd understand his struggle. She appreciated his honesty.

"Maybe you should take some time off," she suggested. "We have plenty of money. I'm worried about you."

"But this is my time. Who knows when it will end? There's always someone younger and more talented around the corner. I have to take the jobs while they're being offered."

"All I want is for you to take care of yourself." Jess rolled over and looked Clay in the eyes. "Promise me you'll slow down if it becomes too much."

"I promise," he said, kissing her softly on the lips. As he gazed into her eyes, he wondered what had happened to him to bring him to this point in his life. He used to only drink a beer or two and have fun, but then the fun turned into something ugly. He wanted to please Jess and put the girls first more than anything in the world, and he couldn't understand why his alcohol addiction pulled on him stronger than his love for his family. He didn't want to disappoint Jess again. He was afraid that the next time would be the last time and he'd lose her forever.

She reached up and brushed the hair from his eyes.

"What are you thinking about? You look a million miles away," she asked softly.

"I'm thinking about how much I love you and the girls and wondering what I'd do if I ever lost you."

Jess smiled. "I'm not going anywhere. I love you so much, Clay. For better or for worse; isn't that what we promised?"

"I'm afraid there has been as much 'worse' as there has been 'better,'" he said.

"That's in the past. We're here together, now. As long as we have each other, we'll be okay."

Clay kissed her again, this time more passionately.

She grinned. "Are you trying to seduce me?"

"Is it working?"

"Maybe if you kiss me just a little bit more," she said.

He was happy to oblige.

Chapter Nineteen

Clay and the girls worked all Sunday morning on the house and furniture before heading to the hospital to visit Jess. Clay had gone into the yellow bedroom as the girls were finishing up and admired their work.

"This looks really nice," he said, glancing around.

The room had a bay window with a seat, a gas fireplace in the corner, and a small bathroom. The yellow was soft and cheery. He looked into the bathroom and noticed it wasn't completely finished.

"I didn't know the bathroom still needed new flooring and a mirror."

"This bathroom and the blue room's bathroom both do," Maddie said. "But then they'll all be done. The other bathrooms are finished."

"What kind of flooring did your mom have in mind?" he asked, getting nervous. He'd never laid any flooring before.

"Tile, just like the other bathrooms. There are boxes of it down in the basement."

"So, I have to finish putting together the furniture for this room and then lay the tile flooring. And it all has to be done by May 26?" Clay asked. "Do I have enough time?"

Maddie shrugged. "Mr. Neilson can lay the flooring if you don't know how. Mom did the other bathrooms all by herself."

Clay's brows rose. "Is that a challenge?"

Maddie smirked. "I'm just saying that if you can't do it, he can."

"Hmm." He knew Maddie was playing him, and he found it kind of funny. "I'll need his help to show me how it's done, but then I'll do it myself," he said.

Maddie shrugged again, but she was grinning.

They all cleaned up and headed for the hospital, stopping for a quick lunch along the way. The girls sat quietly beside Jess's bed. Maddie was reading a book for English class, and Jilly was playing a game her father had downloaded on his phone for her. Clay put fresh water in the vase of lavender that they'd brought last week. No one had sent new flowers this week, and it saddened Clay. Jess was going into her sixth week of being comatose, and people were already forgetting about her.

As he sat down, Jilly looked up at him with questioning eyes.

"Daddy? If Mom doesn't wake up, ever, then are you going to stay here and still run the B&B?"

Maddie's eyes snapped up from her book, and she glared at her sister. "Don't say that in front of Mom. Of course she's going to wake up."

"But what if she doesn't?" Jilly whined. "Everyone keeps saying Mom is going to wake up, but she hasn't yet. What if she keeps on sleeping, like Sleeping Beauty? I just want to know if Dad will stay and run the business so we can still live here."

Maddie looked angry, but she held it in and stared at their father, waiting for his answer.

"Jilly, dear. We're working on the house so it'll be ready for when Mom wakes up. I'm going to believe that she'll come back to us and run the business."

"But you're a guitar player," Jilly said. "Are you going to leave us again to play music?"

He sighed. They'd had such a good weekend. He didn't want to get into this today.

"Jilly-bear, let's just wait and see what happens."

"So, you are going to leave us as soon as Mom wakes up," Maddie said, glaring at him. "And if she doesn't? Are you going to drag us to live in LA so you can work?"

"Why are we even talking about this right now?" he said, exasperated. "I'm not going anywhere. We're working on the house, and I'm living here. All you're doing is upsetting your-selves about something that hasn't happened yet."

"But Mom isn't waking up," Jilly said, tears filling her eyes. "She just keeps lying there. I just want to know what will happen. I don't want to move. I want to stay here, where my friends are and my swimming team is."

Clay dropped to his knees in front of Jilly and took her hands in his. "Sweetie. You're tired. We've worked hard this weekend. There's no need in getting upset right now. Let's just take it one day at a time, okay? That's the motto I live by to stay sober, and it will work well for all of us as we wait for your mom to wake up."

She sniffed and nodded but didn't look convinced.

"Can we go home now?" she asked softly.

Clay looked up at Maddie. "Do you want to go home now too?"

"Yes."

They all said good-bye to Jess. During the car ride home, Jilly fell asleep. He'd been right—she was worn out and needed rest.

Once they were home, Clay carried Jilly to bed and covered her up. He went downstairs and found Maddie in the kitchen having a bowl of cereal for dinner. Leaning against the counter, he watched his twelve-year-old daughter, who seemed so much more grown-up than her age. He supposed that all he'd put her through in the past, and now this horrible experience with her mother, had made her grow up faster than she should have. He felt sad that he was part of the reason for that.

"What?" she asked, eyeing him.

He held back a chuckle. She sounded like the teenager she'd soon be.

"I was just thinking, that's all."

"About what?"

"It's all too much for Jilly, isn't it? Having to go to the hospital every day and watch her mother lie there, not getting better. It's getting to be too much for you too."

"Maybe," Maddie said, setting her spoon in her empty bowl. "I know it's hard on Jilly. She's only seven. She should be playing and going over to friends' houses and having fun."

"What about you? Is it getting hard for you to go there too?"

"A little. But I want us to be there when Mom wakes up. I'm willing to wait it out until the day Mom is better. I don't know how much longer Jilly can stand it, though."

"Where do you get your strength from?" Clay asked, in awe of his daughter. "Certainly not from me."

"Mom says I'm stubborn. Maybe that's what it is instead of strength."

Clay laughed. "Well, you can be that too. But so can I." After a moment, he said, "You know, even before we were married, I asked your mom what she'd name a baby girl if we had one. She said Madison. She told me the name sounded strong and confident, and that girls needed to be strong in this world to survive. And you know what? Your mom was right. You turned out to be all those things, and I couldn't be any prouder of you than I am right now."

Maddie blushed. "Did Mom really say that?"

"Yes. She had your name already picked out. She always knew what she wanted."

"So, what would Mom want now? What would she want us to do?"

Clay took a deep breath and exhaled. "That's a good question. She wouldn't want you or Jilly to be upset, that's for sure."

"Then why don't we go every night to see her for one more week, and after that, maybe cut back a bit," Maddie suggested. "For Jilly's sake."

"Okay. That sounds like a good idea."

Maddie walked toward the kitchen door, then turned and looked at her father.

"This doesn't mean I'm giving up on Mom. I just don't want Jilly to be upset. But for the record, I still believe that Mom is going to wake up."

"Me too," Clay said. "Me too."

* * *

Monday morning after the girls left with Eileen for school, Clay headed to the hospital. On the drive, he decided to offer to carpool the kids to school and help Eileen. He doubted she'd let him, but he should try. He'd recently received a check from the insurance company for Jess's totaled car. The adjuster had also had the air bags checked and explained that they weren't faulty; they just hadn't deployed due to the car not hitting the

186 | Deanna Lynn Sletten

exact spots that would make them open. That had stunned him. He'd never known that cars must hit certain trigger spots in order to deploy air bags. He thought about buying Jess a new car; he could use it to drive the kids back and forth to school. He didn't think she'd mind if he picked it out. She'd want him to use a safe car.

If I'm going to be the girls' main caregiver, then I'd better step up. That thought scared him, though. Did it mean he'd given up on Jess if he started filling her shoes? But if Jess didn't wake up for a long time—or, God forbid, ever—wouldn't she want him to take over? Decisions were difficult during times like these. He wished he were more sure of himself, like Jess had always been. She'd always believed in him more than he ever had.

Once at the hospital, Clay sat down beside Jess and held her hand.

"What should I do, Jess? I want to believe you're coming back to us, but it's getting tougher every day. And life keeps moving forward without you. The girls need to move forward too. They can't sit here every day and wait. Emotionally, it's getting hard for them. And I know that you wouldn't want that. But then, I don't want to leave you behind, either."

Entwining his fingers with hers, he thought about the many times they'd held hands over the years. Walks on the beach, in the mall, under the table at a restaurant. It was so natural for them to hold hands, neither gave it a second thought, and sometimes they'd both be surprised to look down and see their hands clasped together. He loved that despite all he'd put her through with his drinking, Jess was still as in love with him as the day they'd married. And he loved her even more as time went on, because she was his everything. His lover, the mother of their children, his best friend. He loved her for still wanting him after everything they'd been through. No other woman would have put up with what Jess had. How could he now make the decision to leave her behind while he and the girls moved forward?

"It's so hard, baby. So, so hard. You have to wake up. You have to. There is no excuse for you not to. I don't want to do this all by myself. I can't do it by myself. Without you, I'm useless. Simply useless. You're the one who holds everything together. How could I ever do what you do?"

Clay laid his head down on her hand as the tears fell. He wished he could crawl onto the bed and hold her close. If she could just feel his arms around her one more time, maybe Jess would feel his love for her and come back to him. He had to remind her how good they'd been together, how even in the bad times, they were always in love. Always.

All he wanted was to hold her and never let her go again.

* * *

2014–2015

In the summer of 2014, Clay went on the road for six weeks with a country band that enjoyed their drinking and their weed. Jess had begged him not to go.

"We don't need the money," she'd insisted.

But he'd really wanted to go. The band was moving up the charts fast, and he'd played on their album, so he thought it would be fun to hit the stage with them for a while.

"You don't have to worry about me," he told Jess. "I've been sober for over a year. I've got this. Nothing is going to tempt me to start drinking again."

Being overconfident was his first mistake.

Clay had a bunk on the band's bus and spent every day in cramped quarters with six other guys who thought nothing about starting their morning with a shot of whiskey. He wasn't tempted by the hard liquor or weed. But when someone offered him a beer one night after a concert, his mouth watered. Clay hadn't been able to attend AA meetings or go running while on the road, and whiling away the hours on a tour bus became monotonous. But he refused the drink that first night and was proud of himself for doing so.

It was two weeks into the tour that his resolve began to fade. He hadn't realized when he took this job that the band members fought constantly over the smallest of things. When he'd met them at the studio months before, they'd seemed like a close-knit group. But now, he found that their constant bickering and outright hostility set him on edge. Every night after playing, they'd go after each other, and it drove Clay crazy. Tension and stress were his triggers, and he knew it, so he hid in the bathroom and called Coop for help.

"Get off that tour, man," his friend told him. "It isn't worth it. Your sobriety is more important than playing with this band."

"But I have a contract. They could sue me if I leave. I can't do that to my family," Clay said, feeling trapped.

"You can't start drinking. That would be worse for your family. Call your agent, and see what he can do to get you out of it."

He did call Jeff but was told it was an ironclad contract.

"Just hang in there. Keep your distance from the others, and stay out of their fights. It's only a few more weeks," he said.

Clay knew keeping his distance on a bus was going to be impossible. Even if he hid in his bunk, he could hear them argue and fight. His nerves grew rawer with each passing day. He needed a release.

Late one night as they filed onto the bus, the manager handed out booze to everyone, telling then what a great performance they'd had. The bass player complained that the drummer played the tempo too fast, the piano player said that the bass player's amp was too loud, and the fighting began. Clay couldn't take it any longer. He grabbed a beer from the cooler and found a corner where he could stare out the window at the passing cars while he drank. One became several, and soon he was passed out in his bunk.

It's just while I'm with this crazy band, he told himself. *I've quit before, and I can quit again as soon as I get home. I can handle this.*

But when Clay returned home, the relief of being away from the band and with his family again didn't stop his need to drink. He fought it hard and lost, day after day. He'd tell Jess he had to work at the studio but instead would go to a bar. Then he'd return home long after she went to bed so she wouldn't see him stumble in.

"You smell like beer," Jess said a few times. But Clay would brush it off and say it was being with all the guys drinking at the studio.

"I wouldn't do that to you again," he'd tell her, hating himself for lying.

When Coop called him to find out why he wasn't attending AA meetings, Clay lied and said he'd found a group closer to home that he was going to. Coop said he understood. He never questioned his sobriety. That was how much his friend trusted him. And Clay was letting him down.

Every time he drank, an array of emotions plagued Clay. He felt guilty for lying to Jess and angry with himself for not controlling his urge to drink. He also felt embarrassed and ashamed over being, in his mind, a loser. Jess deserved so much better than him. But his shame and anger only fueled his need to drink, making it impossible for him to quit on his own.

In August, Jess's grandmother became ill and was hospitalized. Jess headed north with the children to be with her, and Clay stayed behind, claiming he had a full calendar of work dates. That was partly true; he was booked for a few dates at the studios. But he also thought he could use the time alone to work on quitting drinking. Yet as each day passed, he always found an excuse to put it off another day. A week later, Jess called him to say that her grandmother had died. She'd had pneumonia and never recovered. It had just been too much for her age and frail body. Clay flew up north to be with Jess as she planned her grandmother's funeral and closed up the house that had been willed to her. Jess wasn't sure what to do with it yet and wanted to give herself some time to decide. Clay understood. The house had been in the family for decades.

His drinking slowed because he couldn't find an excuse to get away and drink. By the time everything was in order and they drove home, he thought he'd kicked the habit altogether. But as soon as they arrived home, he fell back into drinking. It was easier for him to drink than to quit. It called to him so loudly, he felt he had no choice. One night in late September, he was so drunk after a studio session that he called Coop to pick him up and let him sleep it off at his place. He rationalized that Jess would think he was at the studio all night—which happened often—so he didn't call and tell her where he was. But when he walked into the house the next afternoon with bloodshot eyes and wrinkled clothes, Jess looked at him with sorrow in her eyes.

"You're drinking again."

"No, no. I had an all-nighter at the studio. You know how

rough those can be," Clay told her.

"I know that's not true. Coop called and told me you were drinking again. You're not going to AA meetings anymore, and you've been lying to me."

Clay let out a long sigh of relief. It was as if he'd been holding his breath for months, and he could finally let it go.

"I'm sorry, Jess. Yes, I've been drinking. But it's under control, I promise you."

It scared him how easily he lied.

He took a step toward Jess, but she backed up.

"Stop lying to me. You've been drinking, and you don't have it under control. Why, Clay? Why would you risk everything to drink again? Why would you risk losing your family?" Jess asked, tears filling her eyes.

Fear washed over him, twisting his stomach and making him feel sick.

"Losing my family? What do you mean? I haven't done anything so bad that I'd lose all of you."

"You have to quit. Now. Go back to AA meetings, go to rehab, do whatever you need to do to quit. I love you, you know I do, but I won't live my life constantly worrying about you. And I won't feel safe leaving you with the girls if I can't believe you're sober."

"You talk like I'm dangerous," he said angrily. "I didn't drive home last night. And I'd never do anything to hurt the girls. How can you think that of me?"

Jess sat heavily on the bed, tears streaming down her face. "I'm tired, Clay. I can't do this anymore. You either have to get sober or leave. That's it."

"Fine!" He grabbed a duffel bag from his closet and started throwing clothes into it. "If you want me gone, then I'm gone!"

As he said the words, he looked up and saw Maddie and Jilly standing in the doorway, their eyes wide.

"Dad? Where are you going?" Maddie asked. She looked terrified from hearing her parents fight. Jilly just looked confused.

It was the sight of his girls that tore at Clay's heart. Jess was right. He couldn't keep doing this to his family. What was wrong with him that he'd choose drinking over his beautiful girls and a wife who made his life worth living?

Holding back tears, Clay set his bag down and walked over to the girls.

"I'm not going anywhere," he said, pulling them into a hug. "I'm sorry if you heard me and Mommy fighting. We're not going to fight anymore." He turned toward Jess. "I'm sorry. I'll do whatever I need to."

He held Jess tightly as the tears fell. He loved her more than anything in this world, and he had almost walked out on her. How could he even think about doing that? All he wanted to do was hold Jess and never let her go.

He asked Coop for help, and for a while, it worked. Clay was able to get sober without going to rehab, and he started running again to relieve stress. For several months, he fought his desire to drink, and it was a tough battle. But by the spring of 2015, he lost that battle again. And in doing so, he also lost Jess and the girls.

Chapter Twenty

Tuesday morning Clay went to the hospital. He thought that he'd spend a couple of hours with Jess, then go looking for a new car. Alex had suggested a couple of car dealerships that he trusted in the city, so Clay thought he'd start there.

He sat beside the bed, telling Jess about Jilly's swimming practice the night before and how well he and the girls were doing after their rocky start.

"You'd be proud of me. I'm learning to cook a few of their favorite foods, and I'm making sure the girls eat healthy meals, not just chicken nuggets." He laughed softly, gazing at her serene face. "We've bought fruit and veggies, and I pack their school lunches every day. Imagine, Maddie is actually letting me do that. And the house is almost finished. I conceded I knew nothing about laying tile flooring, so Alex is doing it for me." He laughed again at this. Maddie had given him a hard time about it, but she was only teasing. "I have a few pieces of furniture left to put together, but that's it. I can't believe you did all the other furniture yourself. You're incredible. But then, we always knew you were so much smarter than me."

He was quiet then, gently caressing her arm as it lay immobile on the bed.

"I miss you so much, sweetie," he finally said softly. "I've been sober for almost two years, and I plan on staying that way from now on. No more excuses. Losing you and the girls was the worst day of my life. And not coming back to you was unforgivable. I was so afraid I'd disappoint you again, and I couldn't bear it. But now, I'm afraid I lost my chance to show you how good things could be. Please come back to me. Please. Give me a chance to make it up to you for all the times I broke your heart."

Clay stood and gave Jess a whisper of a kiss on the lips. "I'll be back later with the girls. I'm going shopping for a new car for you. I hope you don't mind. I'll try to buy one I know you'll love. Bye, sweetie."

As he was turning to leave, he noticed Jess's hand move. Then he saw her body begin to shake all over. Panicked, he ran to the door.

"Nurse! Nurse! Come in here!" he hollered.

A nurse came running, took one look at Jess, and rushed to get a doctor. Within seconds, the room had filled with nurses and the on-call doctor, all working frantically around Jess. A nurse took hold of Clay's arm and pulled him from the room.

"Please wait here," she told him before rushing back into the room.

A few minutes later, Dr. Bradbury hurried past him and into the room. Clay paced the hallway, feeling helpless. He wondered if Jess had had a seizure, or something worse. He was beginning to panic when everyone began filing out of the room.

A nurse walked up to him. "Dr. Bradbury said you may go in now."

He thanked her and hurried into the room. Jess was lying peacefully on the bed.

"What happened?" Clay asked as he drew closer to the doctor.

"Your wife had another seizure. It was more severe than the last one, but the good news is that she's still breathing on her own."

Clay let out a sigh of relief. "Is there any bad news?"

"I'd like to run a brain scan again, just to make sure there isn't any new damage. Otherwise, all seems to be the same."

Clay ran his hand through his hair. "Doctor, please be frank with me. Do you see any chance of Jess coming out of this coma?"

"I can't answer that. I wish I could. There doesn't seem to be any reason for her to still be comatose. Let's wait for the new scan to see if anything has changed."

"And if it has?"

"I can't tell you anything until then. I'm sorry." The doctor paused before continuing. "There is something I'd like to discuss with you. It's time we moved your wife to a long-term care facility. She will receive excellent care, and I'll still continue on as her physician if you so desire. She needs a place where caring for long-term patients is their expertise."

Clay stared blankly at the doctor. "You mean, like a nursing home?"

"It's similar, but most of the patients there have brain injuries or are comatose."

"So, you're saying there's nothing more you can do for her?"

"I'm sorry, Mr. Connors, but it is the best option for her now."

The doctor told Clay that he'd bring him information about a few care facilities and that he'd like to move Jess next week if a space could be secured. Clay barely heard what the doctor said. In his mind, the doctor was giving up. This was a step closer to admitting that Jess might be in a coma for a long time.

He left the hospital in a daze. He no longer had any desire to hunt for a car. He drove through the city, then along the coast. His mind wasn't on driving, so he stopped and climbed down a steep path to a beach cove. The path was well defined, so he knew that many a surfer had walked down its rocky length.

Clay walked along the shore, thinking about everything that had happened today. Putting Jess in a long-term care facility felt like giving up. Was she doomed to lie there for years, withering away and growing old? Would the girls grow up without their mother? And where did that leave him? Could he raise the girls alone, without Jess's innate intuition for what was right and what was wrong? That scared him to death.

Everything was happening too fast, and he wasn't prepared to make these types of decisions. Parenting the girls by himself short-term was one thing, but being their only guidance through life was terrifying.

The afternoon shadows grew long, and Clay knew it was almost time for the girls to return home. The girls would expect to go to the hospital and see their mom. As he climbed up the path, he worried how to tell them about what had happened today. And how would they feel when they heard that their mother would be moved to a long-term care facility? What would they think?

He needed more time to sort out how he felt before he talked to his daughters.

Clay called Eileen and asked her if she'd mind watching the girls until he came home.

"Of course. You sound distracted. Is everything okay?"

"It's been a rough day," he told her. "I have a lot to think about."

After he hung up, he drove around aimlessly. He passed first one bar and then another. His hands began to shake, and his mouth grew dry. It was stressful times like this when he wanted a drink more than anything else in the world. One drink to clear his head. One drink to give him the release his tense mind needed so desperately.

Clay had no idea how long he drove in circles, fighting the urge growing inside him. The sun slowly faded in the sky, and he watched as the moon rose. One drink. Just one.

Clay couldn't fight it any longer. He pulled into the parking lot of a small bar and went inside.

* * *

Two hours passed as Clay sat at the bar. Men were playing pool, and the clack of the balls on the table echoed in the room. A beer sat in front of him, and music blared from the jukebox on the other side of the room. But for Clay, it was all just background noise as he stared at the golden liquid in his glass.

He became aware of a man sitting down in the stool next to him.

"How's it going, Clay?" a deep voice asked. Clay knew instantly that it was Alex.

"How'd you find me?" Clay asked, still staring down at his beer.

"Eileen said you sounded a little desperate on the phone, and she was worried. I drove by a few bars to look for you before stopping here."

"I guess that's the first place an alcoholic looks for another alcoholic," Clay said.

"Actually, I'd hoped not to find you in one. So, how many have you had?"

Clay glanced over at Alex. "This is my first one."

"Doesn't look like you took a drink out of it yet."

"I haven't."

"How long you been sitting here?"

"I don't know. An hour. Two, maybe."

"Two hours and fifteen minutes," the bartender piped up. "I only timed him because I thought it was strange he only stared at it."

Alex's lips curved into a small smile. "I wonder if that's some sort of record."

The bartender shrugged. "Seems strange to me." He walked on down the bar.

"Come on," Alex said to Clay. "Let's sit in a booth over there."

Clay followed Alex over to a corner booth by the wall. Alex waved the waitress over. "Can we get some wings with medium sauce and two coffees, please?" He turned to Clay. "They have the best wings here. I bet you haven't had any dinner yet."

"I haven't."

"Want to talk about what's wrong?" Alex asked.

"Jess had another seizure today. I was there when it happened. It frightened me."

"That's rough. I'm sorry. Is she okay?"

"The doctor is going to do another brain scan to make sure. At least she's still breathing on her own. That's one thing to be thankful for."

"So, what made you come here?"

Clay rubbed his hand over the back of his neck. "The doctor wants to put Jess in a long-term care facility. As far as I'm concerned, that means he's given up on her. Just thinking about

Jess being in a coma for years, or forever, scares me to death." He looked at Alex. "What will I do without her? How will I raise the girls alone? I'm lost without Jess."

"I'm sorry. I really am. But you have to stay positive. Did the doctor say she might not wake up?"

"No, but he won't give any definitive answers."

"Then we have to keep believing that Jess will wake up," Alex said with certainty.

The waitress came with their coffee and wings. Clay hadn't thought he could eat a bite, but they smelled so good, he tried first one, then another.

"How did you know they serve such good wings here?"

"Some guys on my crew told me. Eileen and I have been here for a quick bite before."

Clay's eyebrows rose.

"Hey, just because I can't drink doesn't mean I can't eat in a bar," Alex said.

Clay chuckled. "I guess not. You're a stronger man than I'll ever be."

"That's not true. I don't know how I'd react if I were going through what you are. You've been doing a great job—with the girls, the house, and seeing Jess every day. You're stronger than you give yourself credit for."

"Until I ended up here."

"But you didn't drink anything. That takes some heavy control."

Clay thought about that. When he'd entered the bar, he had intended to drink. But after it had been put in front of him, he couldn't make himself take that first sip. He'd thought about Maddie and Jilly and how disappointed they'd be in him. And then he'd thought about Jess and how he had to be the responsible one now. How could he let her down again?

"How am I going to do this without Jess? I want to believe she'll wake up, but if she doesn't, how will I fill her shoes?"

"There's only one answer to every difficult question," Alex said. "One day at a time. That's how you'll do it. The same way you stopped drinking. The same way you made it to two years sober. One day at a time. Anything else is too overwhelming."

Clay nodded. "You're right."

They finished eating and drank down their coffee.

"Thanks, Alex. I don't know too many people who'd drive around to all the bars in the area looking for someone. You're a true friend."

"Anytime. Are you ready to go home?"

"Yeah. I am. And thanks to you, I'm going home sober."

Alex shook his head. "No, that was all you. You can do this, Clay. No matter what happens. You have it in you to take on whatever comes your way."

"Thanks."

Maddie was at the door the minute Clay walked in to collect his girls from Alex and Eileen's house.

"Where were you?" she asked, sounding concerned.

"Let's go home and talk."

He thanked Alex again, and Eileen for caring enough to send him. Once home, Clay led the girls into the living room to sit down.

"What happened to you tonight?" Maddie asked. She didn't sound angry, only upset.

Jilly stared at him, waiting for an answer.

"I'm sorry I ran out like that," he said. "And that I didn't take you to see your mom tonight. I won't lie to you. I had a rough day and sort of lost it. But everything is fine now. I won't do that again."

"Did something happen to Mom?" Maddie asked.

"Your mom had another seizure this afternoon. She's fine and is still breathing on her own. I was there when it happened, and it frightened me. But I promise, she's fine."

To his surprise, tears filled Maddie's eyes. She turned away and swiped at them, but he knew she was crying.

"Madds? Are you okay?"

"I'm fine," she said, her voice trembling.

"Jilly? Maybe you should go upstairs and get ready for bed. I'll be up in a minute," he said.

Jilly nodded and stood up.

"How about you, kiddo? Are you okay?" he asked Jilly.

She smiled. "Yeah, I knew you'd come back."

Clay's heart swelled. He hoped he could live up to the blind faith that Jilly had in him. He led her to the staircase and gave her a hug. "I'll be up soon."

Jilly slowly walked up the stairs.

Going back into the living room, he sat down next to Maddie. "What's wrong, Madds?"

She had managed to stop the tears, but her eyes looked red and tired. "I thought you'd left us. That you'd had enough, and you weren't coming back." Her voice shook as she spoke.

"Oh, Madds." Clay hugged her, and to his surprise, she let him. "I'm so sorry. I never thought of leaving you and Jilly. I promise you that. But I did almost ruin everything, and I'm more determined than ever now not to do that. I'm here, and I'm not going anywhere. I promise."

Maddie pulled away and looked up into his eyes. "I know I've been mean to you and that you've been doing everything you can to make me believe you won't leave. But tonight, I was scared you'd left and it was my fault. I don't want to push you away. Jilly and I need you."

Tears welled in his eyes. "Now I'm going to cry," he said, trying to smile. "Do you know how long I've waited to hear you say that? I love you so much, Madds. And Jilly. And your mom. I couldn't even think of a life without all of you ever again. I'm sorry I didn't come back to you the last time, but I'll never do that again."

"I believe you now," Maddie said.

"That is music to my ears," Clay said, wiping away his tears.

"What about Mom? Is she really okay?"

"I'm trying to be as honest as possible with you girls. I only know what the doctor has told me, and so far, she's okay. But there are going to be some changes. He wants to move her to another place where they'll take care of her. It may be for the better. I'm not sure."

"They don't think she'll wake up anytime soon, then," Maddie said.

Clay shook his head. "I'm hoping that's not true, but we'll keep praying for the best."

They stood and walked to the staircase, ascending it slowly. Jilly was already in her pajamas and had brushed her teeth. Clay kissed her and Maddie good night. When he reached their bedroom door, Maddie called to him.

"Dad? Maybe you could sleep in Mom's room from now on, until she gets home."

"That sounds like a good idea. I'll move in there tomorrow," Clay said, understanding how big a step that was for Maddie to offer. "Good night."

Walking downstairs to he room, he thought about all he could have lost tonight if he'd taken even one sip of beer. He was thankful he'd had the strength not to. His girls needed him more than ever, and he wasn't going to let them down. Standing in the darkened house after turning off the last of the lights, Clay said softly, "Come back to us, Jess. We need you."

Chapter Twenty-One

The next night at the AA meeting, Clay stood when it was his turn and shared his story.

"I almost lost my sobriety last night," he said. "I would have lost everything if I'd taken that first sip. I'm thankful now that I didn't. And a good friend reminded me how I will be able to get through this difficult time: one day at a time. It's a simple answer, but one that I had forgotten. I have to apply it to my entire life, not just my sobriety. We all should."

Everyone nodded in agreement, and after the meeting, a new member came up to Clay and thanked him for sharing.

"You're right," she told him. "It is such a simple phrase, but it has a powerful message. I'm going to try to apply it to everything in my life too."

Clay was happy that his words had made an impact on her.

Earlier that day when Clay had visited the hospital, nothing had changed. The doctor told him that Jess's brain scan had looked fine.

"No swelling or extra fluid," he'd said. "We should still be hopeful."

But Clay didn't feel hopeful. He felt as if each passing day that Jess was in a coma meant she was drifting further away from them.

That night he slept in Jess's room, comforted by being surrounded by her things. It was a cozy room with a four-poster bed, a brick fireplace in the corner, and a private attached bathroom. Photos of their life sat on the mantel: their wedding picture, baby pictures of the girls, and family photos from throughout the years. He was in many of the photos, proving that Jess had still believed in him, still believed he'd come home to them.

No matter how far away you go, or no matter for how long, you'll always come back to me. Jess's words reverberated in his mind. He just wished he'd come home sooner.

* * *

The next day, Clay visited the hospital and was greeted by the doctor as he was making his rounds. The doctor said he'd left a few pamphlets about care facilities that had openings in Jess's room for Clay to look through.

"I know you'll have to work with your insurance company over this, but once you've made a decision, please let the staff know," the doctor said. "These rooms fill up fast, so we'll want to get her in as soon as possible."

As Clay sat with Jess, he tried looking over the pamphlets, but it was hard. The places seemed nice, but they were still care facilities. He felt like he'd be putting Jess away in a corner somewhere like you would an unwanted piece of furniture or old toy. He hated that thought.

Clay pushed those thoughts out of his mind as he picked the girls up from home and took them to visit Jess. Jilly immediately went to her mother's side and told her about her day in school.

"Jerrod and I chalked out a hopscotch on the sidewalk at recess, just like you showed me, Mom," she said. "We were in the middle of a game when some of the other boys came by and started making fun of Jerrod for playing a 'girls' game. I could tell he was upset, so I said he didn't have to play anymore, but it made me sad. But my other friend, Ashley, came over to play instead, so I guess that was okay."

Clay smiled at his daughter's retelling of her day, but he saw that Maddie was rolling her eyes. He supposed that, to a twelve-year-old, Jilly's problems weren't all that important. He walked over to her and said softly, "You were seven once too."

"I suppose," she said with a long, drawn-out sigh.

They went to the cafeteria for dinner and then back to the room for a few more minutes with Jess. Clay knew he had to seriously look at the choices for care facilities and then talk to his insurance company. He dreaded it but decided to do it the next morning, when the girls weren't within earshot.

"What are these?" Jilly asked, picking up the pamphlets that Clay had left on the windowsill.

He instantly regretted he hadn't put them away. He hadn't wanted to mention Jess's moving to Jilly yet, but now he was forced to.

"The doctor suggested that Mommy might do better living someplace else," he said carefully. "A place where they are experts at taking care of people in Mom's condition."

Jilly opened each one and looked at the colorful pictures. There were pretty lawns and trees and big dining rooms. The rooms looked like hospital rooms, only a bit nicer. In many of the pictures, elderly men and women sat in wheelchairs.

"Does Mom have to go to a place like this?" Jilly asked,

staring up at her father.

"Yes, for a while."

"But everyone there looks old. Mom isn't old."

Clay's antennae went up at the small whine in Jilly's voice.

"Yes, sweetie, some of the residents will be older, but I'm sure there will be younger residents who live there too."

"Why can't Mom stay here? I like it here," Jilly whined.

Clay walked over to where Jilly stood with the pamphlets in her hand and kneeled down in front of her. "This is a nice place too, Jilly-bear, but the new place is specifically for people who need long-term care, like Mom. I'm sure they'll be really good to her there."

Jilly's face crumpled. "I don't want Mommy to go there. She won't get better there. I want her here!"

Tears filled her eyes and fell in streams down her cheeks.

Maddie came over and tried to help. "Jilly, don't cry. Let's go to the candy machine and get something we can share. Like M&Ms."

"No!" Jilly yelled. "I want Mommy to stay here. Don't let them move her, Dad. Please? I want her to stay here." Her voice was shrill as her tears now came in a torrent. Clay picked her up and held her.

"Get her stuff, Madds. We need to leave."

Maddie grabbed Jilly's backpack and began shoving things inside it. She picked up the book Jilly had left near Jess's hand on the bed. "Dad?"

By now Jilly was crying hysterically. Clay was trying to calm her down, but nothing was working. "Come on, Madds. Let's go."

"Dad, look," Maddie said, pointing to the bed.

He walked toward the door. "Let's go, Maddie!" he shouted over Jilly's cries.

"DAD! LOOK!" Maddie yelled.

Clay spun around to see where Maddie was pointing. Jess's arm was lying on the bed, but it wasn't still. It was reaching out, taut, as if grabbing for something.

"Mom's moving," Maddie said. "Look, Mom's moving!"

Jilly's sobs stopped, and she stared at her mother. Jess continued to reach, almost frantically, as if trying desperately to touch something.

"Run and get the nurse," Clay told Maddie, who didn't have to be told twice. She left the room in a hurry, calling for a nurse.

Her tears forgotten, Jilly said, "Mommy's moving. Mommy's waking up!"

Clay set her down and hurried over to his wife. Her face looked strained, as if she were upset.

"Jess? Jess, honey. Can you hear me? It's Clay. Please wake up, sweetie. We all want you to wake up."

A nurse rushed into the room and stopped when she saw Jess's arm extended and hand moving.

"I'll call for the doctor," she said, leaving the room.

Maddie reappeared and wrapped her arm around Jilly as they both watched their mother. Clay continued to speak to Jess softly, caressing her cheek with the back of his hand as he spoke. "Wake up, honey. Please wake up. Maddie and Jilly and I are here. Come back to us."

Slowly, Jess's brow smoothed, and her arm relaxed and lay back down. She grew quiet again, just as she'd been before Jilly had started crying. But she didn't wake up.

A doctor came into the room with the nurse, asking what had happened. He wasn't Dr. Bradbury and wasn't familiar with Jess's case, but he listened as first the nurse, then Clay, described what had happened.

He checked her pulse and blood pressure and looked at her pupils. "She seems calm now. I'm afraid it was just a spasm. That happens sometimes."

Clay walked up to the doctor. "Couldn't she have been reacting to something? My daughter was crying at the time it happened. Maybe Jess could hear her and was trying to wake up."

The doctor looked at him with compassion in his eyes. "I wouldn't rule anything out, but I also wouldn't put too much hope into it, either. Your wife is peaceful now. There's no sign of distress, no irregular heartbeat. I'm sorry, Mr. Connors. I wish there had been more to it."

Disappointment fell over Clay.

The doctor left, and the nurse rechecked Jess's vital signs, then turned to Clay and the girls. "I saw it. It was more than a spasm. Keep believing."

"Thank you," Clay said. "That means a lot to us."

He and the girls sat there a while longer, hoping for another sign that Jess would wake up, but none came. Finally, holding hands, the three left.

* * *

When they returned home that night, Clay was both physically and emotionally spent. He gave Jilly extra attention when he tucked her into bed to make sure she was okay. After he made sure the house was locked up and all the lights were off, he walked heavily up the stairs to Jess's bedroom and dropped on the bed. He was too tired to take off his clothes, too stressed to do anything more than stare at the ceiling and think about Jess.

The doctor was wrong. It hadn't been just a spasm. If that

were the truth, then why didn't Jess have them regularly? Why did she have one at the exact moment her daughter was crying? To Clay, there was only one answer—Jess had heard Jilly crying, and she was trying to find her way back to comfort her. A child in distress is the worst sound any mother could hear, and Jess was no different. Jilly's tears had caused her to react. Clay knew in his heart this was true.

So, how could he get Jess to respond enough to wake up?

Jilly's distress hadn't brought Jess out of her coma because she'd stopped crying, and Clay had spoke soothingly to Jess until she calmed down. If the crying had continued, would Jess have woken up? He hated the thought of using stress to bring Jess back. It had to be something else. Something that would tear at her heartstrings and make her want to push herself to wake up.

Then Clay remembered the song.

They had tried playing the CD they'd made of "Colour My World" before, and it hadn't caused a reaction. But what about live music? What if he, Maddie, and Emma played live for Jess? Clay knew that song was special to Jess. Would it be enough to get her to react?

He had to try. He finally fell asleep, feeling hopeful.

* * *

Clay spent Friday morning on the phone talking to his medical insurance and to the managers of two of the facilities the doctor had recommended. He made appointments to visit both facilities on Monday, because he had to see them before making the decision—one of the hardest decisions of his life.

One facility that he was leaning toward was an hour and a half away, while the other one was closer. But he had to place

Jess's care first over the distance, though he knew it would be hard for the girls to visit often if she were in the farther one. They'd be relegated to seeing their mother on weekends, maybe even only once a week. He hated that. But he had to do what was best for Jess.

Clay called Eileen and asked her if she thought the high school would lend them a small electric piano over the weekend.

She knew the music teacher well, so she didn't think it would be a problem. "I'll pick it up when I get the kids. Are you planning a recital?"

Clay chuckled. "Kind of. Would you be willing to bring Emma and her violin to the hospital tonight after dinner? Bring Jerrod and Alex too, if they'd like to come. There's something I want to do for Jess."

"Well, now I'm intrigued," Eileen said.

Clay told her his plan, and she agreed it was worth trying. "We'll be there."

Instead of going to the hospital that afternoon, he opted to do some work around the house. He changed the beds, did some laundry, then made a grocery run. These simple tasks kept his mind focused so he wouldn't stress about tonight. *One day at a time,* he kept telling himself. When the girls came home, he had everything in order and was ready to face the evening.

* * *

Clay told the girls his plan while they were out to dinner. "Let's play Mom's favorite song live for her and see if we can get through to her. I'm not guaranteeing she'll wake up, but we can at least try."

Maddie agreed it was a good idea, but Jilly looked skeptical.

"We played the CD for Mom, and nothing happened. Why would this do it?"

"I'm not saying it will do the trick, sweetie, but it's the one thing we haven't tried. I believe that your mom reacted to your crying last night, and that's why she moved. This time, I'm hoping she'll react to hearing her favorite song played by those she loves most. We just have to try."

"Okay," Jilly said, brightening. "Let's try."

Maddie carried the electric piano and Clay carried his guitar into the hospital. Jilly followed, her eyes alight with excitement. The Neilsons were all waiting for them in the reception area, and Emma had her violin case.

"Thanks for coming," Clay said to all of them.

"We wouldn't have missed it," Alex said.

"Let's go to Jess's room." Clay led the procession down the hall.

When they entered Jess's room, a nurse was checking her vitals.

"What do we have here?" the young nurse asked. "Looks like a concert."

Jilly piped up. "We're going to play music for my mom."

The nurse smiled at her.

"That sounds nice. I'm sure she'll enjoy it," she said as she left the room.

Maddie set the piano on the rolling bed tray and plugged it in. She'd written the music on song sheets for Emma, and she placed it on the piano's music tray. Clay pulled out his guitar and slipped the strap over his shoulder, while Emma took her violin out and went to stand next to Maddie. Everyone positioned themselves around the room. Alex and Eileen stood together at the foot of the bed, while Jilly stood beside her mother, and

Jerrod sat on the window ledge. Tonight, the musicians weren't the main attraction; Jess was. All eyes were on her, waiting to see a twitch or a blink, any indication that she could hear the music.

Clay walked closer to the bed, bent down, and placed a light kiss on Jess's forehead.

"Everyone you love is here, sweetie," he said softly. "We all want more than anything for you to come back to us. Please try. Here's your favorite song, our wedding song, to pull you to us."

Straightening up, he nodded at Maddie to begin. Jilly glanced up at him, and he gave her an encouraging smile. Maddie began, playing each note beautifully. Soon, Emma joined in, the strings of her violin adding sweetness to the song. Then Clay started to play, strumming softly. The music was rich and full. It drifted and floated through the air, magical and enchanting, sweet and heartwarming. And then it flourished as Clay began to sing.

"As time goes on, I realize, how much you mean, to me."

The door opened softly, and nurses tiptoed in. A doctor joined them. Everyone stood, transfixed, as the music flowed and Clay sang. Tears filled his eyes as the words touched his heart. How perfectly the words described this moment in time.

Memories enveloped him. The first time he and Jess met. Their first date. When he first touched his lips to hers. He loved her dearly then, and so very much now. As he stared down at Jess, he mentally urged her to wake up. To come back to him and the girls and fill their life with joy again.

The words ended, but the song played on. Clay glanced at Maddie and saw that she too had tears rolling down her cheeks as she concentrated on playing. Emma played on too, every note perfect. *How proud her parents must be of her right now,* Clay thought. And Jilly, his sweet little Jilly-bear. Her eyes were focused only on Jess, waiting, hoping, for her mother to wake up.

Maddie and Emma played the final notes, and all went silent. No one moved. Everyone stared at Jess. But she just lay there, silent, unmoving.

A collective sigh filled the room as if everyone had been holding their breath. Clay looked up and saw Eileen wiping away tears. The nurses and doctor all looked as disappointed as Clay felt. They had hoped for magic to happen too. They had hoped for a miracle. The doctor and nurses quietly left the room.

Jilly looked up at her dad. "Mommy didn't wake up."

"I know, sweetie. I'm sorry. But we tried."

Eileen walked over to Maddie and Emma and wrapped her arms around their shoulders. "You both played beautifully. Every note was perfect. I'm sure Jess heard it and loved every moment of it."

"We can hope for that," Clay said, sitting down in the chair and placing his guitar in its case.

"Maybe you could try again," Jilly said hopefully.

He reached out and pulled his younger daughter to him, kissing the top of her head. "We will, Jilly-bear. Another time. We won't stop trying. But I think we should pack up and go home now. We'll come back and see your mom tomorrow."

All the hope and expectation everyone had felt now fell to the floor, waiting to be swept away. Maddie boxed up the piano, and Emma placed her violin in its case. No one spoke. There was nothing left to say.

Eileen led the procession out of the room with Maddie, Emma, Jilly, and Jerrod following close behind. Their heads were bent, and their shoulders drooped with disappointment.

Alex placed his hand on Clay's shoulder. "Don't lose hope."

Clay nodded. He wasn't sure how much hope he had left.

After Alex left, Clay gazed down at Jess one last time. Next week, after he'd chosen a care facility, she'd spend her days there. It seemed so final. Like he'd already lost her.

He bent down and kissed her lightly on the lips. "I love you more than anything in this world, sweetie." Picking up his guitar case, he walked to the door.

"Clay?"

He stopped when he heard the soft noise. He shook his head. *No, I must be hearing things.*

"Clay?"

This time he'd heard it clearly. Someone was saying his name.

Turning, he gazed at Jess. Her eyes were open, and her head was turned in his direction.

"Jess?" He hurried closer to the bed. Jess's head moved as he drew nearer. "Jess!" He put his guitar down and ran to her side.

Her lips turned up in the slightest smile.

"I knew you'd come back to me," she whispered.

Tears sprang to his eyes. "Yes, my love. I came back. And so did you. And I promise I'll never leave you again." He reached down and cupped her face before placing a gentle kiss on her lips. "I love you, Jess. You're everything to me." She gazed up at him and smiled.

Excitement coursed through him.

"I have to tell everyone!" he said, running to the door and pulling it open. "Maddie! Jilly! Everyone! Hurry! She's awake! She's awake!"

The group had been standing glumly in the hallway waiting for him, but as soon as they heard the news, they came running in. Maddie and Jilly led the way. The girls went to their mother's bedside and stopped. Jess's eyes were closed.

"Mommy?" Jilly said hesitantly.

Jess's eyelids fluttered; then she opened them and gazed at

her youngest daughter.

"Jilly-bear," she whispered. "Maddie. Oh, my sweethearts."

The girls began to cry as they crawled up into the bed and hugged their mother. Jess wrapped her arms around them as tears fell down her cheeks too.

Eileen and Alex stood, teary-eyed, their arms around each other. Emma and Jerrod stared in amazement, happiness marked clearly on their faces.

Soon the room was filled with nurses and the on-call doctor. They all stared at Jess in wonder. A miracle had indeed happened.

Epilogue

"Tell me again how it happened," Jilly said, cuddled in bed beside her mother at home two weeks later. "Tell me how Daddy woke you up."

Jess laughed softly as she pulled her daughter to her. "You've heard it so many times, you can tell it yourself."

"But I want you to tell it," Jilly said.

"Okay," Jess relented.

Maddie walked into the room with her mother's lunch on a tray. "Jilly, are you pestering Mom again? You know she needs her rest."

"I just want to hear the story again," her sister insisted.

Maddie rolled her eyes, but she sat on the end of their mother's bed to listen too.

Jess began to speak. "As I lay there in bed, I could hear music playing, but it sounded far, far away. I recognized my favorite song, our wedding song. I felt like I was lost in a thick, dense fog. I tried pushing through it to get to the music, but it was so hard. My body wanted to sleep, but my mind wanted to find the music. Then, the song stopped, and I lost all hope of ever finding it."

"And then Daddy kissed you?" Jilly piped up.

"Let Mom tell it," Maddie said.

Jess laughed softly and continued. "I started to fall back down through the fog, back toward the darkness. I thought maybe I had been dreaming the music, like I'd dreamt so many other things. Just as the darkness had almost enveloped me, I felt someone brush my lips in a soft kiss. I heard your father say, 'I love you more than anything in this world.' That's when I knew the music had been real. I had to return. I had to see for myself that your dad had come back."

"And you woke up! Just like Snow White!" Jilly exclaimed.

"Or Sleeping Beauty," Maddie added.

"Or Rip Van Winkle," Clay said, chuckling, as he entered the room.

"Yuck! No one kissed Rip Van Winkle," Maddie said.

He shrugged. "I couldn't think of any other fairy-tale princesses."

"And now we all live happily ever after," Jilly said. "Dad's home, Mom's awake, and we're a family again."

Clay sat on the bed beside Jilly. "Yes. Now we live happily ever after."

Jilly beamed at him.

"But first, you have to let your mom rest and get better," Clay said, lifting Jilly from the bed and setting her on the floor.

It was Jess's turn to roll her eyes. "Rest? I slept for six weeks. Wasn't that enough?"

"You heard the doctor. He said you have to take it easy and work your way back to normal. Otherwise, I'm sending you back to the hospital so they can tell you what to do."

"No hospital. Staying there for a week after I woke up was enough for me," Jess said. "I want to be home with my family."

Her eyes shone when she said that, and Clay's heart melted at the sight. He was so thankful to have her back, and to have his family back. He was taking the summer off to be with them and try to make up for lost time. Eventually, he'd return to playing, but he only wanted to do studio work from now on. No more road tours. No more being tempted to return to drinking. He had his family and his support group here, as well as their amazing neighbors, Eileen and Alex, to keep him on the straight and narrow. And he didn't want to veer from that path ever again.

Clay turned to the girls. "One more week, and the first guests arrive. Are we ready?"

"As ready as we'll ever be," Maddie said.

"I'm ready," Jilly said.

Clay grinned. Maddie had done a wonderful job of filling in for Jess and getting the house ready. And she was still giving orders. Maddie was going to be a great help to her mother, now that she felt a part of the business.

"I wish I could make breakfast for our very first guests," Jess said, looking disappointed.

Clay caressed her cheek. "Let's see how you feel next week. I don't want you to overdo it."

She gazed up into her husband's eyes. "You're babying me, you know. I'll be fine. In fact, I plan on feeling well enough by Monday night to go to the middle school concert. No one is stopping me from hearing Maddie and Emma play my favorite song."

"You were lucky. You had a private concert," he said as he kissed the top of her head.

"Yuck. Come on, Jilly. Our lunch is ready downstairs. Let's leave them alone." Maddie turned and headed out the door with Jilly at her heels.

Clay grinned at his girls as they left. "It's nice to be home," he said, returning his gaze to Jess. He sat down next to Jess, pulling her into his arms.

"Yes," she said softly. "It's nice to be home."

About the Author

Deanna Lynn Sletten is the author of THE WOMEN OF GREAT HERON LAKE, MISS ETTA, MAGGIE'S TURN, FINDING LIBBIE, and several other titles. She writes heart-warming women's fiction, historical fiction, and romance novels with unforgettable characters. She has also written one middle-grade novel that takes you on the adventure of a lifetime. Deanna believes in fate, destiny, love at first sight, soul mates, second chances, and happily ever after, and her novels reflect that.

Deanna is married and has two grown children. When not writing, she enjoys walking the wooded trails around her home with her beautiful Australian Shepherd, traveling, and relaxing on the lake.

Deanna loves hearing from her readers. Connect with her at:
Her website: http://www.deannalsletten.com
Blog: http://www.deannalynnsletten.com
Facebook: http://www.facebook.com/deannalynnsletten
Twitter: http://www.twitter.com/deannalsletten

Printed in Great Britain
by Amazon